FAR FROM HERE

Far From Here

a novel

Eden Alson

ARBITRARY PRESS

New York

*Here is my hand, my heart,
my throat, my wrist. Here are the illuminated
cities at the center of me, and here is the center
of me, which is a lake, which is a well that we
can drink from.*

—Richard Siken

For Mom and Dad. I couldn't do it without you.

PART ONE

Now

All I see is white.

White walls. White sheets. White curtains. A white desk with white plastic legs. A window that faces bleached white bricks. A white bed. A white shelf piled high with folded white shirts and pants.

"Hello?" I yell.

My voice hangs there for a moment, sucked up by the whiteness.

The doors to the room burst open and two men in blue rush in, a third man in a white coat behind them. The man in white holds a long needle in his rubber-gloved hand. I try to squirm away, screaming and thrashing my arms. The two men in blue hold me down as I kick at them wildly, slamming my foot against one of the side rails of the bed. There's a jolt of lightning in my foot, searing pain. The man in the white coat sticks the needle in my arm. In seconds, all the energy and pain drains out of me and the world fades away.

When I open my eyes again, I'm in the same white room. I feel like I'm swimming up from underwater, my vision wet and blurry. My foot throbs. When I look down toward the end of the bed, I see that my foot's propped up on a folded towel and wrapped in a heavy white bandage, except for my toes, which stick out. I wiggle them, just to make sure they're actually mine. When I was little and fell down, my sister, Summer, would ask me where it hurt, and wherever I pointed to, she would kiss it. Sometimes I'd tell her, "Everywhere," so she'd give me a bunch of kisses. But I doubt my sister would be able to kiss the inside of my head or inside the heavy white cast encasing my foot.

"Sir, please try to understand."

I blink my eyes open. I must have passed out again. The man in the white coat has returned. He's speaking to a man with dark circles under his eyes who's dressed in tan trousers and a blue, collared shirt.

"Legally she's mine," the tired-looking man in the blue shirt says. "I'm taking her home."

I make a sound somewhere between a moan and a whimper. They both turn in my direction.

"Hannah." The Tired Man seems to be talking to me, which is weird because that's not my name.

"My name isn't Hannah," I say just before everything fades out again.

"Hannah."

I open my eyes, praying that this time they'll stay open.

I'm still in the white room but not in the bed anymore. Now, I'm in a chair, with my wrapped-up foot on a leg rest. Someone must have propped me up, but I don't remember that happening. The Tired Man sits in a chair across from me, looking like he's on the verge of sleep.

"Hannah, do you remember me?"

I don't understand, and as much as I desperately want to tell him that my name isn't Hannah and that I know that he's not like me, that he's a disbeliever, I say nothing. Disbelievers shouldn't know your name.

"I'm your Uncle Nathan."

This is obviously a lie.

"Your mother was my sister," he says.

My mother's only family was us.

"I'm taking you back home with me to New Jersey."

I don't know where New Jersey is, but I know it's not home.

"Hannah, please. Talk to me."

Just as he says this, I start listing to one side—I can feel myself about to crash to the floor. The Tired Man must see it, because he rushes towards me, yelling, "Hannah!"

This time when I come to I'm sitting in a chair with wheels the size of hula hoops, hurtling down a long white corridor. The Tired Man's behind me, pushing, breathing hard. I try to put my good foot down to stop us, but my sock only skids across the floor.

A moment later, we're outside in sunshine so bright I have to squint. The Tired Man stops pushing. He picks me up and hoists me over his shoulder. I protest, but it's pointless. I'm too weak to stand on my own, much less get away.

He carries me to a car that's parked at the curb. The only other car I've ever known is the battered green pickup truck we used for grocery runs. This is much smaller. The Tired Man opens the door and dumps me into the seat, reaching behind my head for a strap which he stretches across my chest, clicking it into place, trapping me. He slams my door shut, circles around to the other side and climbs in. He turns the key. A moment later, we peel away from the building with a sharp squeal.

He says nothing as we drive past buildings taller than anything I've ever seen, up a ramp, and onto a giant road where we join four lanes of whizzing traffic. On the other side of the divider, four more lanes of cars speed toward us. It's terrifying but also weirdly hypnotic. I've never been on a road like this. Really, I've never been on a road. The Tired Man stares straight ahead, fully concentrated. Twenty minutes later, he turns down a ramp and stops the car outside a large glass building that's shaped like a giant umbrella. Overhead, planes are angling up into the sky. Summer told me about planes. She used to say that all she ever wanted was to fly. On boring days, she made paper airplanes and threw them around in our room. The sound of these planes is like a windstorm in the desert.

The Tired Man gets out of the car and talks to a man in a red shirt and cap behind an outdoor counter. The two of them come back, wheeling another chair like the one I was in before. They lift me into it, even as I squirm, lamely trying to resist.

The man in the red cap, with the Tired Man at his side, pushes me in the chair toward these enormous glass doors that slide open as if by magic. We stop inside by a row of blue boxes with screens in the middle. The Tired Man taps at the screen of one, then waits until the blue box spits out two pieces of paper. Grabbing them, he thanks the man in the red cap, then pushes me toward the back of a line of people, all of whom grip long handles attached to bags on wheels. The Tired Man seems agitated, glancing at his watch as the line inches forward. We're midway to these conveyor belts up ahead, where I can see people taking off their shoes and emptying their pockets. A bored-looking woman in a blue suit jacket and frilly scarf warns us to have our tickets ready and to make sure we don't have any liquids or gels in our bags. The Tired Man talks to her, gesturing at me several times. I hear him say the words "wheelchair" and "security" but it's hard to understand why he's so agitated.

Even though her bored expression never changes, whatever it is he's saying seems to have an effect on this woman, because she takes us out of the line, leading us past the people ahead of us, who shoot us dirty looks.

A man in uniform waves us around the horseshoe-shaped booth that other people keep having to stand in. On the other side of it, another man in uniform passes a wand over our bodies, then motions us to proceed. We walk down a long ramp, past numbered sitting areas, stopping when we get to one numbered A9. The Tired Man slides me and my chair into a space between two of the anchored chairs and sits down beside me.

Something about the way he sits, legs spread apart, looks sad to me. He's hunched over, elbows resting on his knees, hands supporting his downcast face. He runs one hand through his hair, which is the same color as mine, reddish brown.

Twenty minutes go by and there's an announcement I don't really listen to over the loudspeaker. "That's us," the Tired Man says, looking up. "That's our flight." He wheels me down a long tube-shaped corridor toward a pill-shaped open door where a smiling woman in a blue uniform greets us.

After the ordeal of getting me into a seat, we sit for what feels like an eternity. And then, through my little window, I see the ground going by, slowly at first, but then with increasing speed. Suddenly, with a lurch I feel in my stomach, we lift up into the air. Outside, the world below gets smaller and smaller, until I can't see the ground anymore, just sky and clouds like giant pillows that we fly straight into.

I can't see God or his angels roaming around from here.

All I see is white.

Four Years Before

U ncle Dan always makes us popsicles on Sundays.

He pours orange juice into ice-cube trays, so the popsicles are square-shaped and make our tongues sting, but we eat them every Sunday without fail.

When we were little, we got them as a reward for good behavior in chapel, but my best friend Sami and I are ten now. We know how to behave. Still, we want our reward. Our little brothers and sisters can't have all the fun.

On Sunday, apart from chapel, we don't do anything. Chores, other than cooking, are called off, because even God rests on Sunday. We're supposed to reflect and relax, but mostly we play. Today, Sami points out that Augur always says, "We shall take this, the last day of another fine week on God's path, to reflect and relax," but Sunday is actually the first day of the new week. Laughing, I remind her that Augur speaks for God, so maybe we should consider that Sunday is the last day of the week. She laughs, too, nodding, because she knows I'm right.

"Truth or Dare?" Sami asks me. We're lying on the ground. She's breathing against my face. Her breath smells like oranges. She extends one hand, reaching toward the sky, fingers dancing. Even on hot, dusty days like this, she can't keep still. She entwines the fingers of her other hand with mine; her dark skin contrasts sharply against my pasty fingers.

Summer taught me the Truth or Dare game. She says that she saw it on TV when we were still allowed to watch things other than the news. Now Sami and I play the game all the time.

"Dare." I say, wiggling so that I can look right at the sun. I suck on my Popsicle stick while she thinks.

"Draw our initials in the ground," she says after a moment.

"Where?" I say, sitting up.

"Right here!"

"Okay." I pull the popsicle stick from my mouth and carve an S and a G into the ground with it. Sami leans over my shoulder. I turn, looking at her for approval. We admire my handiwork. Her fingers are sticky and orange like mine.

"Cool, now our initials will be here forever," she says.

"Just like us," I say.

"Yeah, just like us."

But in the morning, when we go back, our initials are gone, blown away by the desert wind.

Now

The Tired Man's house is like all the others on the street where he lives. Two stories tall with a short driveway leading to a garage door. His house is the only yellow one and there are daisies in the window boxes. It's nice. Cheery, almost.

All I want to do now is get away from here and get home somehow. On the plane, when the fog cleared and the drugs wore off, I panicked. The Tired Man tried to calm me down, but I was inconsolable. It's safe to say the other passengers were less than thrilled.

Augur always said that we should fight as hard as we could if we ever got captured by the disbelievers. And if that didn't work and we couldn't get away, we should kill ourselves. Right now, I don't see an escape route. Plus, one of my feet is trapped in a thick plaster cast that runs up to my calf.

The Tired Man gets out of the car and starts down the path to his front door. Is he gonna leave me in here to overheat and die like a dog?

But then he stops and turns back, looking at me through the glare of the windshield, shaking his head. Every muscle in my body tenses up under his gaze. He opens my door, and says in a soft voice, "I'm sorry, I'm so fried I forgot you can't walk. I'm going to have to carry you again."

I don't respond and don't move.

"Hannah, please, do you have to make this difficult?"

Why does he keep calling me Hannah?

"My name is Gracelyn," I mutter, instantly filled with regret for telling him.

"What?" he says, leaning into the car.

"My name is Gracelyn. Not *Hannah*." My voice is full of venom.

"I'm sorry, Gracelyn," he says, putting emphasis on my name. "When you were born, your mom called you Hannah, because it means...well, Grace. But things like that change."

"Gracelyn means blessing." What a stupid thing to say.

I try to remember that I'm not supposed to talk to him. I shift my gaze so I'm looking straight ahead and not at him.

Stay focused. Keep your cool. He's just trying to ingratiate himself so you'll let your guard down.

He sighs, leaning against the side of the car. "Can you please swing around so I can lift you up?"

I don't answer him, but I do what he asks, anyway. What else am I going to do?

For a moment, as he picks me up, I catch sight of my reflection in the car window. It's startling. My hair's cut unevenly just below my chin. I'm wearing a gray baggy sweater and gray pants, eyes hollowed out, cheeks sunken and ash-colored. I look weak, defeated. My memory of my reflection—from the one solitary mirror in our quarters—I looked nothing like this. My hair used to be annoyingly long, heavy to tie up, always tangled in the morning. Yet I miss it. It's almost as if a limb was severed.

Your hair will grow back. Focus.

There's a dying daisy in one of the window boxes. Sad—like the Tired Man. He pulls keys from one of his jacket pockets and struggles, while carrying me, to open the door.

Inside, first thing, I'm hit with a wave of heat. There's a hissing radiator in the corner. The Tired Man nods toward the stairs. "I'll take you to your room. You must be wiped out... from everything."

I am, though I don't want to let him know that.

He struggles up the stairs with me, then down a hall to a room at the far end. It has a single bed near a sloping window, a flowered chair, and another door. He carries me to it and lays me down on the bed. He says, "You can sleep if you like. I know this must be overwhelming. I'll bring up some lunch later. Okay?"

I don't answer, but he leaves, closing the door behind him.

I'm alone.

Fetal position, hands cupped by my chest like fish fins. I'm too tired now to think about escaping, plus there's the matter of my broken foot. I'll think of a plan later. After I close my eyes.

A girl sits on the edge of my bed.

For a moment, I wonder if she's even real. Her hair is bright purple, like a fairy or an alien.

"Daaad," she yells, scrunching up her nose, "she's awaaaake."

She's holding a cell phone. I've never seen one in real life. Hers is pink and sparkly, with a sticker on the back.

"I'm Lauren," she says, looking at me strangely. "What's your name?"

"I'm—" No, no more telling anyone anything.

The Tired Man appears in the doorway. "Hi, Gracelyn. Feeling any better?" I can smell the cigarette smoke on his clothes. I don't answer him or even really look at him.

"Would you like some lunch now?" It sounds more like a plea than a question.

I'm starving, but I just shrug.

"I'll take that as a yes." He nods his head towards the door, and his daughter—Lauren, I guess—gets up. She gives me a funny look when our eyes meet. I look away.

The two of them leave, and I lie there on the bed, staring at the ceiling. Are they going to poison me? Or maybe they'll just torture me, dangle food in front of me like I'm an animal.

Twenty minutes later, I hear footsteps. They're heavy, so I know it's the Tired Man. He comes in and sits at the foot of the bed. He's got a tray that has a glass of orange juice and a grilled cheese sandwich.

"Here you go, Gracelyn." When I don't respond, he gets fidgety. He says, "Well, I guess I'll just leave it here and let you eat it in peace." When I still say nothing, he shakes his head, sighs, and leaves.

An hour later, he's back. Looking at the tray, which I haven't touched, he gets so sad I think he's going to cry. "Gracelyn, are you sure you don't want something to eat? You must be hungry," he says. There's that pleading voice again. I should never have told him my name. Stupid, stupid, stupid.

"I want to help you," he says. "But I can't help you if you starve."

Why am I here?

"You're safe here, Gracelyn, even if you don't know it yet."

Where's Summer?

"Just please eat something."

No.

That word. "No" wasn't allowed at home, but it's allowed here, and I want to scream it from the rooftops until someone hears me. No. No. No. "No!" I scream aloud.

He looks at me, fear in his eyes. Good. He's afraid of me.

His daughter appears in the door, probably to see what's happening. I scream "Nooo!" again, directing it at her this time. She steps back out, terrified.

The Tired Man decides he's had enough as well, following her into the hallway.

I can hear them from in here. Maybe they don't realize.

"She's fragile, Lauren."

"She's scary is what she is."

"Lauren!"

"What? It's true, isn't it? She screams like a crazy person when you try to talk to her. You know that's not normal."

"She's your flesh and blood, young lady, and she's been through hell. You saw all those terrible images on the news just like I did. Think about what that must do to a person."

Lauren's voice gets quiet and sad. "I'm sorry, Dad."

"I know..." Their footsteps move away, growing softer.

I lie back on the bed.

So, these people, they're scared of me.

Good.

Four Years Before

Everyone waits differently.

Sami waits by fidgeting. She picks at her clothes and her hair, squirming in the pew. Her mom, Aunt Salma, keeps grabbing at Sami's wrists to stop her. Summer hums to herself, picking at her cuticles. She's always been a hummer. But lately the song has changed. Aunt Elizabeth waits by scoping all the women, checking to see if they look better than her this morning. I wait by sitting on my hands and chewing on my lower lip. Augur always says that patience is a virtue, but Sami says that's just his excuse for making us wait around for him all the time. I'm the only one with whom she would dare share such a thought.

Suddenly, the door to the chapel bursts open and he struts in. The way the sunlight hits his back creates a halo around his whole body.

Sami hates these meetings, but I like them because I enjoy seeing him. His name is actually Randolph, but we all call him Augur. Even his kids and wives.

He walks up to the lectern, lays down his bible and smiles over the crowd. "My family. Thank you for your patience. Our Lord had a lot to say this morning."

A few people chuckle.

After leading us through a prayer, he tells us a bit about what's happening on the outside (nothing good). But what we're all really waiting for is his sermon—where he'll tell us what God had to say.

"Today the lord was very voluble about the children among us, those children who are on the brink of becoming adults."

"The girls, in particular, are getting older." His eyes flit toward me. I feel my face get hot. "I don't have to tell you that with age comes temptation. You all must enforce the lord's rules on your little sisters, your daughters, your nieces." I look over at Sami, who is self-consciously picking her shirt away from her chest. "They are becoming women before your very eyes, and that can be a dangerous thing."

His gaze shifts away from me, but my face still feels hotter than the center of the earth.

"All of this to say that you all must be wary of what is happening behind the eyes of your children. You never know where demons may lurk."

After chapel, we have confession. As I get older, I'm hating confession more and more. It's starting to feel awkward to spill all my secrets to someone I eat every meal with.

"Good morning, Gracelyn," Augur says when I sit down outside of the broom closet. There's a little hole drilled in the door so he can hear us. I don't think he can see out of it, but he always knows who it is.

"Good morning." I cross myself. "I was envious of Fawn on her birthday. She got a hairbrush that I wanted. Also, I talked back to my sister. And I let my mind wander during last night's sermon." I rock back and forth in my chair.

"Anything else?"

It felt like you were talking about me in the sermon this morning. "No. I'm sorry for all my sins."

"For your penance, two rounds."

Only two today. That's good. I cross myself again. "Thank you Augur. Amen."

"Go in peace."

At the door, I let in the next person, then go and sit in the pews. We're meant to pray while we wait for our penance, an old tradition from the outside. I clasp my hands together and whisper, "Our father who art in heaven…"

Now

I've never slept more in my life.

Back at home, we had a strict waking schedule. No matter how long the sermons went, we had to wake up at seven in the morning, if not earlier. Here, I've woken up after nine-thirty every day. It feels sinful, but I can't stop.

Nightmares without fail: fire, blood, people screaming. Usually Summer is there, and I hear Augur's voice too.

I don't know what happened before the white room. I know people died, I know there was a fire, maybe a bomb. But I can't remember how I got out, or what happened to Summer...or Sami.

It's cold here. Sometimes too cold to get warm even under a blanket. We lived in a desert, hot and oppressive during the day, full of dust and the smell of sweat. Here it smells like rain.

Lauren comes in every so often to read. I think she's supposed to be "keeping an eye on me," but it seems like I still freak her out too much for her to start a conversation. More often, it's the Tired Man who comes in. He usually sticks it out for twenty minutes trying to talk to me.

It's true that I've given in and eaten, but that was only because the hunger pains grew too intense to ignore. Soup and crackers. No poison so far.

When I crack the door open, I can hear the news coming from the television downstairs. Most of what I hear has no meaning for me, although from time to time, I hear the odd familiar name.

ATF Commander John Helicon.

Oliver Jacobs and Gina Locet.

Randolph Milly.

So something did happen.

Something big.

The doorbell rings occasionally, and I see flashes of light through my window and hear the people outside, talking. But the Tired Man never lets them in or responds.

I think they're here about me.

I haven't asked about Sami or Summer yet. I want to, desperately, but I don't. I don't want to show or tell them anything.

Time goes by like it's not going by at all. Though sometimes it feels like the sun is racing the moon.

Lauren comes in with purpose today, holding her phone, which seems to be connected to her ears by a white plastic cord. She's smiling.

"Do you like music?" she asks, taking a plug out of one ear.

Obviously, I like music. Who doesn't? I wonder if this is a trap, if she's going to plunge the plug into my eye or choke me to death with the cord? Disbelievers are dangerous. If they see a weakened servant of God, they'll try to lead them astray. And once you've strayed, there might be no way to save you.

I know she's just a child. She can't be much older than me. But it's hard not to think of a phrase from the Bible: *For even Satan disguises himself as an angel of light.*

And yet I still let her sit on the bed.

"This album?" She gently places one of the plastic pieces in my ear. It feels strange, unnatural, but I don't flinch. "It's the shit. You'll see." She clicks a little button on the side of her phone, and then one on the screen.

Suddenly, I hear what sounds like a drill cutting through glass. I'm pretty sure it's supposed to be music, but I recoil reflexively, yanking the plastic out of my ear with a weird little whimper. Embarrassing, but hey. Lauren looks so guilty it almost makes me feel better.

"Sorry," she says, jabbing at the screen. "Didn't realize." She puts the phone down on the bed and leans back, bed hugging her legs to her chest.

If her father sits like he's sad, she sits like she's anxious. Sami used to sit like that.

"You seem really nice," she says after a while. That seems like a stretch, or a lie. "You have a nice face."

Something about the phrase "You have a nice face" makes me want to laugh. I don't, but the impulse is there.

We sit in silence a little longer. Then Lauren leans a bit closer to me and reaches out as if she's about to touch my hair. "Red is the coolest hair color," she says. I disagree. Unnatural though it is, I think her hair color is way cooler than mine. "But whoever cut your hair did a choppy job. Do you want me to fix it?"

I've never ever seen anyone cut hair, but I certainly don't want her putting scissors anywhere near my scalp. I shake my head.

"Um, maybe you want some new clothes then? I have a bunch that might fit you."

I shake my head again, even though I don't really want to wear these sweatpants anymore.

"That's okay. Maybe tomorrow." She gets up and leaves.

The next time, she's holding a pair of scissors. But they're thinner and smaller than kitchen scissors. There are some clothes slung over her arm. In her other hand, there's a plate of cookies. She offers them to me and takes one for herself. I don't take one, but my mouth waters.

"Want me to cut your hair today?" she asks, chewing.

I refuse again. I don't remember too well what my hair looks like, but I'm sure it can't be *that* bad.

"Okay," she says. "Maybe tomorrow."

She comes back the next day with the same supplies and again asks if I want a cookie and if I want her to cut my hair. I make it clear I still don't want either.

Over the next two weeks, she comes back every day without fail at 3:30 pm, bearing sandwich cookies, scissors and clothes. Each time I turn her down, she says, "Okay, maybe tomorrow."

Even if it's some bizarre form of torture, I admire her persistence.

I assume she's my age, maybe a little younger. Under the purple, her hair is dark brown. I know from hearing her talk to her dad and on the phone that she has friends named Violet, George, and Anna. I also know that she leaves for school at 8:15 a.m. on a yellow bus and arrives home at 3:10 p.m. on the same bus. Every day at dinner, Lauren says that whatever they are eating is her favorite. Last week, a black car pulled up in front of the house, and Lauren got into it. She didn't come back for two days. I think it was her mother in the car. When she came back, her visits with me lasted fifteen minutes longer, I guess to make up for missing the previous two days.

I'm on high alert, but around Lauren things feel a little calmer.

By halfway through the second week, it feels like layers of my brain are peeling off, and I need to escape this place. It makes more sense to wait until my foot heals, but I'm impatient.

And frankly, I'm scared of what's going to happen to me if I wait around any longer.

Although my window doesn't open, this room is connected to a bathroom, which is connected to another bedroom, which I'm pretty sure belongs to the Tired Man. So while Lauren is gone, and the Tired Man is downstairs, I seize my chance.

I start my pathetic journey through the bathroom and into his room. I'm thinking: Window, roof, porch, road, airport? This is a poorly thought-out plan, but I'm not going to let that stop me. I've gotta get out of this damn house.

Ignoring the menagerie of knick-knacks in the Tired Man's room, I make a beeline for the window. Hard to open, but I manage.

A few feet to the left of the small windowsill is the roof above the porch. I take off my clunky walking boot, a process I've mastered from taking it off to go to bed at night.

Using my good foot to climb on the dresser, I make my way out onto the sill. It's a precarious position, for sure. I have one chance to reach that roof, and if I don't make it, well, that's one way of getting out of here.

I think I can reach it by stretching out my leg to touch the porch roof while holding onto the overhang above me, but that may be a bit optimistic considering my condition.

What the hell. Nothing ventured, nothing gained.

Except that when I try, my broken foot slips, and for a terrifying, stomach-lurching moment, I think I'm gonna fall. I don't, though. I get onto the roof in one piece, then take a moment to calm myself. *You're fine. That was the scary part.*

When I'm breathing normally again, I slither down one of the porch posts and limp my way to the street.

Relief. Euphoria, even. I make my way down the block, glancing back at the house, which looks quiet and small now.

Just as I'm beginning to get my bearings, a woman with a gray afro approaches me. "Hey," she says, blocking my path. "Are you allowed to be out here by yourself?" She looks behind me. "Does Nathan know where you are?"

"Um..." I stammer. She grabs my arm. I try to shake her off. But she's too strong. Either that—or I'm too weak.

"That's what I thought," she says.

She drags me back to the Tired Man's house. He opens the door, looking completely freaked out to see me. "Jesus," he says. He thanks her profusely. She shrugs, saying she was glad to be of help. After he closes the door, the Tired Man marches me back upstairs, without saying anything.

He locks the door to my room and the bathroom door that leads to his bedroom.

So I'm trapped here. Perhaps forever.

Four Years Before

ugur calls together a meeting tonight. I expect a sermon, but some of my aunts whisper that it might be a marriage announcement.

Even though there's no jewelry, fancy clothing, makeup or hair styling products allowed here, the women do their best to make themselves look beautiful for Augur.

They brush their hair until it glistens in the light of the setting sun, and they pinch their cheeks to give themselves a blush. They cut slits in their skirts to show off their legs. It goes against the unwritten rules, but none of the men seem to object.

I don't know why they want him to look at them so much. I don't think he's particularly handsome. Not that what I think matters. I'm not old enough to marry Augur, anyway. Something has to happen first that no one will explain to me in full detail.

Every girl here is promised to him. Anyone without his blood is fair game. If God declares that Augur is to take a wife from a pre-existing marriage and make her his own, then she has to leave that marriage. And no one is allowed to have children except Augur. That rule is fairly new, only about ten years old. But God said that the only way for someone to be born completely holy is to be descended from a prophet. Sometimes Augur teases that the children here that aren't his are somehow tainted. While *he* might think that's funny, it makes me feel like I'm a piece of gum on the bottom of his shoe.

Summer and I sit down in the fourth row, next to Aunt Elizabeth and Uncle Payton. I can't take my eyes off Aunt Elizabeth's blindingly shiny hair. She gives me a look, but I can't stop staring.

"Gracelyn, you're being incredibly rude," Aunt Elizabeth scolds.

I'm tempted to say something about her hair, but Summer pinches my arm and apologizes for me.

Aunt Elizabeth huffs and moves along down the pew. She's only a few years older than Summer, and the two of them have a half-friendship, half-rivalry, that I've never been able to untangle.

Augur stands at the lectern, the bible open in front of him. He holds his arms out, and everyone falls silent. "My brothers, sisters, my children, my family." He looks over us with an expression full of love. "Our all-loving God has given me knowledge, the knowledge that I am to take another wife, who will bear me beautiful, faithful children." His gaze seems to focus, and suddenly, he's looking right at me.

No. I can't be his wife. I thought this wasn't allowed. I don't want to marry him. I can't. *I can't.*

"Summer, join me here. The Lord has chosen you."

I look at Summer, flabbergasted.

She doesn't even look back at me, just stands and joins Augur at the lectern. He puts his arm around her, and she smiles. I can hear jealous murmurs from my aunts. Aunt Elizabeth plays with the ends of her hair. She seems ticked off.

Looking at Summer, I realize that everything's about to change. Summer will move to the women's quarters, she'll have children, different jobs around the compound—and I'll have to fend for myself without her.

Summer gets the chance to bear beautiful children and marry the holiest man alive and all you can think about is yourself?

Augur has his arm wrapped around Summer's shoulders, squeezing her close. To me, it looks uncomfortable, but she looks happy all the same.

Listening to Augur finish his sermon, my head spins. All I can think about is the wedding, and what I'm going to do during thunderstorms.

It's dark outside when we're let out. Instead of Summer leading me and Sami back to our quarters like normal, Aunt Salma tells Fawn to take us. Fawn is only two years older than we are, but I guess she's old enough to walk us places in the dark. Aunt Salma could take us, but all the women are staying behind with Summer, to coo at her and be jealous, I suppose.

Excited by her sudden power, Fawn takes both of our hands and practically yanks us along, all the way back to the children's quarters.

When we get back to the children's quarters, Fawn starts ordering us around, even reminding us to brush in a circular motion. Sami rolls her eyes, but we both do as we're told, since we don't really feel like arguing.

I get into our bunk bed. It's wide enough so that I can go down the ladder and climb in with Summer when I have nightmares. But I guess that'll be over soon.

The door swings open. Summer.

A few of the older girls swarm around her, giggling about Augur and the wedding. She answers their questions quickly. I can tell that she's crashing. After a while, she tells her new fans that she's tired, and she climbs into bed with me.

I'm clutching Harry, my stuffed bunny, and she puts her arm around me, hugging me tight. When the lights go out, I start crying, tiny sobs that only Summer can hear.

"I know, I know. It's all gonna be fine, baby-girl. You'll be okay."

But it's not me I'm worried about.

Now

On the fifth day of the third week, when Lauren asks if she can cut my hair, I give in and nod yes. I am desperately bored after my escape attempt.

She smiles so wide I think her teeth might fall out. "Okay, wait a second." She runs out to where the bathroom is and comes back with a towel, a thin comb and a clip.

I limp gingerly to the chair by the window. She tosses the towel over my shoulders and starts to comb out my hair. I can feel how uneven it is.

Sami used to braid my hair when it was too hot to wear down. She was good at it, better than any of the older women.

Lauren makes her first cut after about three minutes of combing. The snipping sound scares me. I feel a tiny clump of hair fall down the back of my shirt. Lauren gasps a little bit. "Ooh—that's short."

I want to push her away, but I don't. I sit still, to avoid her doing anything that we'll both regret.

I look at the plate of cookies on the little table in front of me.

I take one.

Just like that, Lauren is done cutting my hair. I guess there isn't much to cut. She flits out of the room for a moment, leaving me to chew the cookie, which I hate to admit is one of the best things I've ever tasted.

"What do you think?" she says, holding up a mirror when she returns.

My hair is short—shorter even than when I caught a glimpse of it in the car window. But it looks better. Less uneven. Lauren has a proud smile on her face. I want to be nice, so I try to smile back, but it doesn't really work, and I end up giving her a weird grimace instead. Somehow, it's enough for her. She says, "You love it. I *knew* you would love it!"

I nod dutifully, continuing to inspect my reflection.

The mirror at home was dirty, smudged with fingerprints, covered in dust. No one ever cleaned it, and there was really no need. Vanity wasn't encouraged. The details of my face have never looked so clear.

My green eyes are dull, like someone sucked the light from them. The bones of my face are sharp. They make me look like a geometrical drawing, no soft edges. The scar above my left eye is more pronounced than I thought it was, and my freckles are lighter than they've ever been. I guess I haven't seen the sun in a while. I don't mind. I'm used to my face being red and peeling. When I look back at Lauren, I can suddenly see how similar we look.

"You okay?" she says.

"I don't know," I whisper.

Lauren looks shocked that I spoke. *I'm* shocked.

"Well," she says slowly, lowering the mirror, handing it to me. "Sometimes it's okay not to know things."

She leaves the room, and I shake out my hair. Some falls onto the sheets. I look at myself in the mirror again, not sure I like what I see.

Two days later, the Tired Man comes to sit in my room, and lightly taps my cast. "We need to get this checked out soon."

He's mentioned this a few times, but now I respond.

"I want to watch the news," I say.

He looks at me like I have two heads.

"I want to know what's going on. And I want to see a list of who survived." It took me a few hours this morning to figure out exactly what I wanted to say to him. I decided that saying "I want" was better than saying "I need" because "need" would show weakness.

He takes a deep breath. "I don't think the news is a good idea. The doctors said that I should keep you far away from the news, at least until they finish investigating."

Finish? It's not over? I feel my eyes watering but blink away the tears. "Okay." *Good. Be complacent, let him think that you don't care about anything.* "What about a list?"

He makes this noise, which sounds like sucking the air between his teeth. "I don't know if I can get that for you, but I'll try. It might not be... complete yet."

They're still looking for bodies?

"Gracelyn—"

I can't. That's enough talking for today.

I put a pillow over my head and hum to myself until I hear the door close behind him. It will be two and a half hours until he comes in again to give me my soup, and at least four hours until Lauren comes in to say goodnight, as she's taken to doing.

I'm alone.

I get up from the bed and take a lame step towards the door across the room. Maybe I'll take a bath. With the cast, it's a bit of a high-risk/high reward situation, but I have plenty of time on my hands.

In the bathroom, I jiggle the handle of the Tired Man's bedroom door just like I do every time I go in.

To my surprise, instead of the handle barely moving, it turns.

Whoa! I open the door a crack to make sure that no one's there. The coast is clear. I'm not stupid. I mean, I might be a little bit stupid. But this time I just want a change of scenery. I'm so bored of looking at the same four walls. I listen, just to make sure the Tired Man isn't nearby, then I slip into his room.

There's a desk to the right, against the wall, with what I think is a computer on it. A bookcase is suspended above the desk. Window above the dresser. Tall closet in the corner. Armchair by the other window.

I start with the closet.

The air inside smells musty, like old clothes. There are big puffy jackets on candy-colored plastic hangers. Thick foam goggles hang by their straps from a nail. On the closet floor, two pairs of brightly colored plastic boots bigger than anything I can imagine anyone wearing on their feet.

It's clear that no one has cleaned inside here for years. There's a dead fly near one of the boots, dust balls in the back corners. I close the door and turn my attention to the desk.

Apart from the computer, there's a tape dispenser shaped like a lizard, pencils and pens in a cup, a blank notebook. Above the computer, there's a bookshelf with some knickknacks and framed photos next to a few books.

This family isn't very organized.

I pull down a random book. "The Adults Are Talking: How To Involve Your Children In Uncomfortable Conversations." The picture on the front is of a sad young boy looking at an older woman.

I put the book back next to a photo of Lauren holding a fish almost half her size. She's hooked her fingers through the gills, and she looks very sheepish. Killing animals is a sin.

There's a photo of the Tired Man, looking less tired—younger, and happier. He's wearing a ridiculous black hat and a long matching gown. He holds a piece of paper. There are two other people with their arms around him, looking very proud. What shocks me is seeing the person on the far left. She, too, looks younger here, but I see it so clearly.

It's my mom.

Though I've only ever seen her in pictures, and in the pictures I've seen she's older, I can still tell that it's her. She's laughing, pushing the hat just off the Tired Man's head. Her strawberry blonde hair is long, windblown. Her dress is sleeveless, her shoulders are freckled, and she's wearing the necklace Summer used to have hanging up next to our bed. Her eyes are partially closed, and her teeth are bright white. Compared to the others who look stiff, formal, and professional, she seems light and free, and looks so much like Summer I almost can't breathe.

I return the picture to the shelf and fall back onto the desk chair. My boot-heel hits the floor hard, and a pain shoots up through my leg, but my mind is racing too hard for it to really bother me.

I remember the Tired Man telling me that he was my mother's brother, but I didn't believe him; I thought it was a ploy. I've noticed how similar Lauren and I look, but I didn't think it meant anything.

It means something now.

The Tired Man is my real uncle. Lauren is my cousin.

They're my family.

Four Years Before

We've had about two weddings every year since I was born. Mostly they're Augur's weddings, but occasionally someone else wants to get married, and we have a small ceremony. I never thought I'd be participating in one of the weddings until my own, but here I am, helping with Summer's.

I'm sitting in the women's bathroom with Summer and a couple of my other aunts, plus Fawn, who is twelve and suddenly obsessed with the idea of getting married. Summer is repurposing the prettiest of all the white dresses we have tucked away in the women's closet.

"All right, you have something borrowed, the dress," says Aunt Glinda, who is obsessively picking at Summer's hair. "Something old, your mother's necklace; something new, the veil; now you just need something blue." She smiles when she comes face to face with my sister. "You look so beautiful."

"Glinda, that's not how we do weddings here," says Aunt Elizabeth, spite in her voice. "Summer looks fine."

"Oh, I know. Let me have my sentimental fun, Elizabeth," Aunt Glinda says, smoothing down the veil with the back of her hand.

"I have something blue!" says Fawn.

Summer grins. "Problem solved! Go get it."

Fawn nods aggressively and bolts from the bathroom. I kick my feet at the floor. They're squished into a pair of scuffed up Mary-Janes that only sort of fit me two years ago. Summer lifts my chin up and looks me dead in the eyes. "Hey, cheer up."

I shake my head, stubbornly committed to not enjoying this day one bit.

"Please, Grace, for me? It's my wedding day." She looks so desperate that I can't help but nod. "Thank you, baby girl." I smile, and she smiles back. Maybe I should be happy that she's happy.

Fawn bursts back through the bathroom door, holding a blue pom-pom glued to a safety pin. Aunt Glinda *and* Aunt Elizabeth are about to object, but Summer's face lights up. "Fawn, that's perfect. Thank you."

Fawn beams ear to ear as the Aunts grudgingly pin Summer's "something blue" to her dress. I can't help but smile, too. My sister looks like a princess.

Just then, the door swings open, and Uncle Hiram stands in the doorway. He's always reminded me of a shark. He has big sharp white teeth, gray hair, and a long face. He's giving us all his shark grin. "Hello ladies." His gaze flit over all of us, and when it reaches Fawn, she quickly lowers her gaze toward the floor. "Summer, you look radiant. Augur is waiting for you."

Aunt Glinda gives Summer's dress a last inspection, then kisses her forehead. "God has blessed you, Summer. I hope you will serve Augur well."

Uncle Hiram offers her his hand, and Summer places her slender fingers in his meaty palm. They walk out the door. Summer glances back one last time before the door swings closed behind her. The room is still full of people, but it seems somehow empty now.

The ceremony is private. Augur and his wife get married in private, in the chapel, and then they come in celebrate with us. It's one of the weirder rituals we have, but no one ever explains it.

Almost all the girls own the same formal dress in different sizes. We found a huge box of them thrown out in town a few years ago. Uncle Dan said it was our lucky day. We could pass these down to each other until we died.

Unfortunately, they're as itchy as if someone cut the fabric from a potato sack, and the color is this ugly light blue. But today we keep it to ourselves because Augur's getting married.

Finally, the doors swing open, and there's Summer, beaming, hand in hand with Augur. The room erupts into cheers and claps. I clap until my hands sting, and Sami whistles, imitating Uncle Hiram, who sits three seats down from us.

For a moment, I think of all the other women who have stood up there, white dresses, strained smiles, maybe flowers in their hair. Sami's mother, with her many earrings, Aunt Hazel, with her long blonde curls. I wonder how Summer feels to be one of many. I wonder if she feels special right now, or if those other women haunt her.

"My family," says Augur, letting go of Summer's hand and silencing the crowd. "Summer and I are now married, and I have no doubt she will bear me good, faithful children." I watch Summer, and when he mentions children, I see a flicker in her eyes, but her smile stays perfect and huge. "Now, we celebrate!" The room once again explodes into cheers.

There's no alcohol allowed here, but we have sparkling cider, and Aunt Helen made her special pasta. Later, Uncle Dan, Uncle Hiram, and Augur play music, and the dancing begins. If you dance with someone of the opposite sex, you have to leave room for the spirit, as Aunt Glinda puts it. Uncle James takes over the lead guitar occasionally so that Augur can dance with Summer.

While I'm watching their first dance, I hear Fawn's voice near my ear. "I want that someday." She says this under her breath, and when I look over at her, her face changes. "With him, of course," she adds, as if she hadn't meant to say it out loud.

Instead of responding, I turn back to watching them dance. My sister looks happy.

Though we're celebrating, we still have a curfew, which means that after about fifteen songs or so, Augur thanks us once again and says goodnight.

Back in our rooms, the older girls are all aflutter about the dancing and the conversations they overheard. "Aunt Elizabeth was so jealous of Aunt Summer," says Juniper, pulling a nightgown over her head.

Allison starts to say something in response, but my ears are suddenly flooded with my own thoughts. *Aunt Summer. Aunt Summer. Aunt Summer.* She's no longer a sister to me. Just one of the many women I call my aunt.

"All right, everyone, lights out!" says Aunt Glinda, coming in like she does every night to make sure we're all behaving and asleep. We scramble into bed, though I get the feeling the chatter won't stop.

Glinda turns out the lights and closes the door behind her.

I don't feel as bad about sleeping alone as I thought I might. I'm so tired from the dancing that I start drifting off almost immediately. But then I hear a moaning noise.

Almost on cue, all the other top bunk girls flip onto their stomachs and pull their pillows over their heads like we've learned to do on wedding nights.

I feel sick.

Now

Against my wishes, and my will, the Tired Man takes me to a doctor. Her name is Dr. Keller, and she has brown fluffy hair. She has a very cheery voice, even when she's talking about the shattered quality of my foot bones. I don't like her. But she does give me a few very important pieces of information.

This whole process will take around a month.

This is what I need to formulate an escape plan—at least one that will work. Once I can walk again, I'm out of here. Just the thought makes me feel better.

One wrench in the plan is what the Tired Man says to me in the car on the way back.

"Gracelyn, the way I see it, we have two options." His eyes are firmly focused on the road. "One is that you can stay with me and Lauren, go to your doctor's appointments, go to a therapist, and eventually be able to call and talk to your friends. But that's only if your therapist thinks you're ready for that and if you're able to accept the fact that you're living with us now and you stop fighting that--and us."

The word *therapist* makes my skin prickle.

"If you can't do that, the other option," he sighs, "is that I take you to a mental health treatment facility here in Jersey and you get better there. Then, hopefully, you can come home and adjust to this new life with us."

Home.

This new life.

Your life.

My life.

At a facility, they'll tie me to a metal chair. They'll pump me full of drugs, show me videos and force my eyes open to watch. And there's no chance I can escape that kind of place—the security will be too tight. At least if I stay with Lauren and the Tired Man, I'll have a chance.

Option one it is then.

The next day, he brings a calendar into my room and hangs it on the wall.

I've been here for almost a month. Fourteen days until the cast comes off...

Lauren still comes in every day and leaves me books. History books, children's books, even a science book. I tear through all of them, waiting for the thing I actually want to read.

Today, the Tired Man comes in with a sandwich instead of soup. There's also an envelope sitting on the tray.

"It's the list," he says.

My heart stops. There's no other explanation for the feeling in my chest when he says those words.

The envelope has a government seal on it. I recognize it from Augur's lectures on different ways the disbelievers would try to infiltrate our home. It's addressed to Nathan Spicer, of 147 Washington Lane, Mendham, New Jersey.

I want to open it. But I don't.

A list with names on it.

I know that mine will be there.

That's all I know.

"Can you..." I don't finish asking, but he seems to understand. He takes the envelope out of my hands and rips the top open.

"It's not going to...help," he stammers. "I don't think. It's short."

"Just read it."

The list is only twenty names long, in alphabetical order. The absence of some names already has me on the verge of tears. But there's one name I do hear.

Samira Green.

I really thought she might not have made it. A wave of relief. But it quickly goes away because he's reached the end of the S's.

"Summer?" I ask.

The Tired Man crouches down to look at me.

"I'm sorry," he whispers.

No. How could that be?

"How?" I mumble. The Tired Man's face looks even more tired.

"It was, um," he coughs. "smoke inhalation." He shakes his head. "I'm sorry."

A loud, guttural sob erupts from my chest. At least that's how it feels. Maybe I don't actually make a sound because the Tired Man just keeps reading.

SummerisdeadSummerisgoneyou'renevergoingtoseeheragainSummerisdead

When he stops—and it doesn't take that long because there aren't nearly enough names—the Tired Man dares to put a hand on my back to try and comfort me. He hands me the list so I can see for myself.

I want to rip it up, throw it out the window, burn it. I want to scream every name that isn't on it to the heavens until someone listens to me.

It's unfair. Just unfair.

If this is God's plan, why does it hurt so much?

Maybe God is just an asshole.

The Tired Man hands me a tissue. There are tears on my cheeks, on my clothes, and on that stupid, stupid list.

"Thank you," I whisper. He takes the tray off the bed and places it on the nightstand.

"At some point," he says, his words deliberate and slow, "once the trials and investigations are over, there will be some sort of memorial." He stops to look for my reaction.

I'm all out.

Augur used to say that death was something to celebrate. If your physical body was gone, but you were true to God, your soul would never really die.

Still, I can't help it. All I want is for their souls to come back to me.

Two Years Before

"Would you die for me?"

That's the question Augur asks us this Sunday.

He poses questions to us all the time, but today, I'm shocked at his tone. No one answers at first. He asks again: "Would you die for me?"

I look around momentarily to see if anyone is going to say something.

"It's not a trick question, folks. Just answer. Don't be shy."

Augur looks at us expectantly, but no one moves.

When new people come here, which doesn't happen often, they're always certain that our leader must be an old man, wise and decrepit like the priests on the outside. But Augur is young. I don't know his exact age, but he can't be more than forty. He has a full head of brown hair, a scruff of facial hair, and striking eyes. Sami has always said they're yellow like a snake's. He doesn't wear priestly robes, they're too hot for this place. He wears jeans and button-down shirts.

For the third time, he says, "Would you die for me?"

This time he looks to the front row. "Hiram. You're one of my oldest companions. One of my most loyal friends and brothers. Maybe you can answer. Would you die for me?"

Uncle Hiram is silent for a moment, but eventually clears his throat and rises off the pew. "Of course, I would die for you, Augur."

Augur smiles. "See, that wasn't so hard." He turns his attention back to the rest of us. "Now everyone else. I ask again. Would you die for me?"

Everyone hesitates, but one by one, they stand and say yes. Since apparently, that's the right answer. They usher their children to stand with them. Summer is one of the first, though she gets to her feet tentatively, motioning for me to stand as well.

I do.

Once everyone is out of their seats, Augur claps his hands together. With every person that gets to their feet, his smile gets wider. "Excellent." He adjusts his shirt collar. "Now, everyone sit back down, here's another question."

We all sit.

"Would you kill for me?"

This time people are faster to stand.

"If you were to kill for me, who would you be killing?"

Almost in unison everyone says, "The disbelievers."

He smiles knowingly. "Really?" He makes us all sit back down. "Would you kill one another for me?"

Slower responses than the second question, but faster than the first. Still, by the end, everyone is on their feet.

"Interesting," he says this as if he's conducting an experiment. Maybe he is. "All right, everyone sit. Today, we're reading from Judges."

And then the sermon carries on as usual. No one discusses what he asked. And no one remarks on people's answers.

Afterward, I go to my bedroom to get my work gloves. Sami comes with me, though she was smart enough to bring her gloves with her to chapel.

"Would you die for him?" I ask abruptly. It's only us two in the room.

We're not looking at each other, which might make it easier for her to be honest. I'm staring at the wall, observing the marks people have carved into the wood.

"No."

Now

The Tired Man tells me he's going out for a few hours. He's leaving Lauren in charge. Before he goes, he asks if I'll feel safe without him here. I feel *safer* without him here. But I don't tell him that.

From my window, I watch his car disappear.

He and Lauren never found out about my trip to his bedroom, which is good, because otherwise I've been incredibly well-behaved since my escape attempt. As a result, they've given me a few more privileges. One is that the door to my room is now unlocked for most of the day. So, while he's gone, I have the perfect opportunity to check out the rest of the house.

Armed with my metal crutches, I take a tentative step out of my room.

There are a few family pictures hanging along the floral-papered hallway walls. One sticks out to me: Lauren and the Tired Man sitting on a couch, hugging. There's nothing particularly special about it; it just makes me a little sad because I don't have any pictures like that with *my* dad—or my mom, for that matter.

I barely remember them. I guess I miss them, but it's really more the idea of having parents I miss. Summer never talked about them. Some people did. Hiram talked about how beautiful my mom was, and Aunt Glinda once said I was smart like my dad. Obviously, none of this really explained who they were. They might as well have been strangers.

Directly across from me there's a sign tacked to a door. "Lauren's room: Come on in!" Sparkly stickers cling to the edges of the sign.

Suddenly, the door opens, and there's Lauren. For a moment, I almost don't recognize her. The purple in her hair has turned pink. She's wearing plaid pants and an oversized t-shirt that says, "We can end gun violence."

She looks at me funny for a second, too. Then a smile breaks across her face, and she says "Perfect, I was just about to come get you for the grand tour."

By "grand tour" Lauren basically means showing me her bedroom, the door to which she opens with a melodramatic flourish.

There's a rug in the center of the room that looks white and fluffy and incredibly soft. When I stand on it, the fluff tickles the bare toes of my non-injured foot. Two enormous bookcases catch my eye. They're full of books and strange objects: colored glass figurines of antelopes and giraffes and elephants; a plastic nun wearing boxing gloves next to a doll with pink hair. There's a plant, which might be fake. Pictures and show posters line the walls.

I've never seen such a decorated room, or a room that so perfectly captures someone's personality. It's like Lauren exploded and her insides—these posters and knickknacks—splattered against the walls.

"I like musicals, obviously," Lauren says, flopping down onto her bed. She hesitates, sitting up to face me. "Do you know what a musical is? Have you ever..." she trails off.

"I know what a musical is." I don't mean my tone to be so sharp, but it shuts her up.

"Okay. Never mind."

Near one bookcase, there's a poster for something called *Kabaret*. It's disturbing. Four black-stockinged high-heeled legs arranged into—what did Lauren's history book call it?—a swastika? With a helmet-haired, mouth-stretched-wide-open face of a woman or a man—it's hard to tell—as the hub around which the legs revolve. I hate it.

Lauren says, "It's the original Polish poster. Dad got it at a vintage shop. Cool, huh?"

No, not cool.

"We should watch it," she says.

"Watch what?"

"The movie, *Cabaret*." Like it's obvious. She pronounces it *cab-ar-ray*. "It's one of my favorite movies. What's yours?"

It feels like she's asking a more complicated question than it seems.

The truth is I haven't watched a movie in a long, long time. And for the record, I'm actually not totally sure what a musical is, though it's too late to ask. The only movie I really remember was one about a fox and a dog that become friends. That was at least eight years ago, before they took away our movie privileges.

I ignore her question, asking her a question instead.

"Where did he go?"

She turns her attention to the window. "School. He's a principal." She looks back at me. "But he's applying for indefinite leave and choosing a temporary replacement." There's a hint of something weird in her voice. Clearly, this is bad and might be my fault.

She bounces up off the bed. "Let's go downstairs. I'll look for our DVD."

Going down a staircase with a broken foot and crutches is tricky and slow. By the time I make it to the bottom, Lauren is already rummaging through boxes in the living room. I explore the kitchen a bit, opening every cabinet I can reach.

On the wall, there are more pictures of Lauren and her father. In one, Lauren is dressed in black and red, growling at the camera, hands curled like claws. A dribble of bright red blood comes from the corner of her mouth. The Tired Man wears a strange, feathered hat, and he's laughing at her. They seem happy. His laughing smile reminds me of my mother. How is it possible to miss someone so much that I barely remember?

"It's cold today," Lauren says, raising her voice so I can hear her. "We can use the fake fireplace and make s'mores." She comes to the open kitchen door, waving a plastic rectangle that's black with pinkish lettering. "I mean, the fire is real," she says. "But we don't have to put logs in there or anything." She retreats into the living room and plops down on the couch. "What are you doing? Come sit." She opens the rectangle and pulls out a disc.

I crutch my way over and cautiously sit on the couch's arm. Lauren has already started the movie during my journey across the room.

While we watch, she comments freely and sings along to the music. After a while, I slide onto the couch and allow myself to get comfortable. It's a very nice couch.

The movie, on the other hand, is *appalling*. I think Augur would have a heart attack watching it—or if he knew I was watching it. It's not exactly pro-degeneracy. But it's still incredibly troubling—evil and scary, like the poster. And yet I can't look away.

My favorite character is Brian. I like his accent. I tell Lauren this about halfway through and she nods thoughtfully.

"I like him too. But he's kind of boring, don't you think? I mean, he doesn't even sing." I'm about to disagree, but then she says, "Although he's actually about to get a little more interesting."

Sally (who Lauren continuously refers to as Liza) and Brian are fighting about something I missed. Then they start discussing Maximilian, which Lauren thinks is a stupid name.

"Oh, screw Maximilian!" Brian says, slamming a cabinet or something.

"Well I do," Sally replies. Poor Brian.

Except that he laughs—genuinely, it seems—which is very confusing, and then he says, *"So do I."*

After that, the characters continue to fight and make up, and then there's a song about a man with two wives. I feel a little sick, and it must show on my face.

"You okay?" Lauren asks, humming the lyrics to the song under her breath.

"When did this movie come out?"

This makes Lauren laugh.

"What's so funny?"

"Just... nothing. You made a pun. I think, like, in 1970."

She doesn't ask why I need to know.

After the movie's over, I feel unnerved. "I don't get it," I say as the credits roll. "What happened?"

She gets excited, as if she's been waiting for someone to ask that question her whole life. She immediately rewinds the movie a bit to focus on the final shot.

"Do you see those guys in the brown uniforms and red armbands?" I nod. "They're Nazis. You know what Nazis are?" I nod again. "So at the start, people are getting them thrown out of the club, the MC is mocking them, so on and so forth. But at the end, because no one did anything about it, they're all over the club." She pauses for a moment, thinking. "And it's all a metaphor or whatever. For fascism." Seeing my face, she sighs. "I don't think we have time to explain fascism. But it's basically just evil. So the moral of the story is don't ignore evil people until it's too late."

Don't pretend there isn't danger everywhere.

"I love Liza Minnelli," Lauren says, quickly changing the topic. "I still think her mom is better, though."

"Who's her mom?"

"Judy Garland."

I don't know who that is.

"You know, Dorothy."

I shake my head.

Lauren looks like I just broke a window. "You've never seen *The Wizard of Oz*?"

I shake my head again.

She thumps the couch with an open hand. "Okay, this is becoming a movie musical marathon. You need to see them all."

Two Years Before

S ummer is having a baby.

I knew this, obviously, but I think the fact may not have registered until just now. And today is possibly the worst day to acknowledge it, because today is the day she's actually having the baby. Augur's baby.

The aunts are in Summer's bedroom, fawning over her and her stomach like it's filled with gold, whispering and gasping and giggling. Sami's parents, Uncle Fredrick and Aunt Salma, owned a clothing shop before they came here, and they've been sewing little baby clothes.

I'm jealous. I can feel in my bones how jealous I am. I never get new clothes. All of mine are hand-me-downs from Summer or some of the other older girls. The jean shorts I'm wearing were Fawn's before she had a growth spurt. I've been having growing pains for a month, so they'll probably belong to someone else soon. My flannel was Summer's when she was my age, and my beat-up boots were salvaged from a dumpster outside a shoe store in town like almost everyone's. The babies don't even know or care that they're getting hand-sewn little outfits. And not even that, no one ever looks at me the way my aunts are looking at Summer and the dumb baby that hasn't even been born yet. It's unfair.

Sami and I have been sitting outside Summer's room for what feels like hours now. Nothing seems to be happening.

"Truth or Dare?" Sami asks.

"Truth," I sigh, leaning back against the wall.

"How are you doing?"

I look away so she can't see the tears springing to my eyes. "I'm okay."

"No, you're not." She grabs my arm and pulls me towards her. "I don't usually cry when I'm okay."

Hearing that, I start full-out bawling, and she wraps her arms around me.

"I think she's going to love it more than me."

"Who could ever love anyone more than you?" Sami draws back. "She's basically your mom, and you were born first. She'll always love you more."

I laugh, and she lets go of me.

"See, it's all gonna be okay," she says. "And I mean, even if she does love it more, which she won't, as long as you have me, everything will be fine. I'll never leave you behind for some dumb baby."

Just as she says that, the door bursts open. Aunt Reina steps out, looking like she's been through a war. Her head wrap is stained with sweat. "Girls, would you like to come in?"

Sami gives me a concerned look.

"Yes, Aunt Reina," I say. She holds the door open for us, and we follow her back in.

Women are crowded around Summer. She's screaming like someone's slicing up her insides. No one is letting us close to her, which I'm thankful for. Just listening is hard enough.

The other door to the room swings open and in walks Augur.

Sami grabs my hand. Everything, even Summer's screams, turns quiet. That's just how things go whenever he enters a room.

"Girls, we are gathered to celebrate the birth of another of my beautiful children, a *true* child of God." He looks at me and Sami, the only children in the room. "No offense." Soft laughs ripple around the room. I suddenly feel about three inches tall. He keeps his gaze on us. "Gracelyn, darling, come here. Look at your sister."

I feel sick. She's in pain. Sami's grip on my hand tightens. But I'll do it. If it pleases Augur, I will do it. I reluctantly let go of Sami's hand and women part like the Red Sea as Augur guides me toward the bed where Summer lies.

Summer's legs are propped up by makeshift stirrups. Between her legs, it's a bloody mess. I squeeze my eyes shut as tight as I can because I don't want to see this. I don't want to see this. Please God, don't make me see this.

"Open your eyes, Gracelyn," Augur says. I shake my head so hard it feels like I might break my neck. His voice lowers to a whisper. "Open them."

"Please, no," I whisper.

"Open your eyes." He says it again, low, in a tone that scares me. "You're a good girl, Gracelyn. I want you to look at the miracle of life and thank God for the opportunity to see it."

Slowly, I open my eyes.

I see what I'm guessing is the baby's head but mostly looks like a dark, hairy blood-matted blob. I watch as it is born, as my sister continues to scream bloody murder. When it finally escapes her body, the baby looks more like a demon than a miracle. Its head is shaped like an ice cream cone, and it moves its arms herky-jerky like an insect. Reina holds it in her arms while one of the other women wipes the blood off its face with a rag. Summer is totally wrung out, her hair plastered to her forehead with sweat.

My stomach bubbles, and my head is suddenly hot. Just as I hear a cute little hiccupping cry, I throw up all over the floor.

Augur turns me around to face him and kisses me on the forehead. "Good girl."

And then he leaves.

After what feels like eons of staring at my own puke, someone remembers that I'm there. Aunt Jane—or maybe Aunt Holly, I'm not sure—takes me to the bathroom, washes off my face, and makes me drink from the faucet. She tells me I'm a good, devoted girl. That Augur is proud of me.

When I go back out after cleaning up, the baby is dressed in a little orange onesie that Aunt Salma sewed the other day. I have to admit that clean, the baby looks adorable. Her face is pink and scrunchy now. Not all the babies born here live. Sami's mom gave birth to a dead baby about a year after she married Augur. She didn't speak to anyone for four months, not even Sami. Thank God Summer's baby is healthy. It would destroy her if her baby died.

Summer cradles her baby in her arms, looking tired but happy. All I can think is, I wish she looked at me the way she looks at her baby.

"Ella, meet your Aunt Grace," she says. I can't help it. The words Aunt Grace make my heart melt a little. "Do you want to hold her?"

"Yeah." I sit on the edge of the bed and accept the baby in my arms.

Ella. It seems impossible that someone so tiny could bear such a strong resemblance to an adult, but she looks like Summer already.

"Summer," Aunt Reina interrupts. "Augur said that she should be called Jenifer. It means 'Fair one.'" Jenifer coos and the excitement on Summer's face drains away.

"Oh. Well, Jenifer is a beautiful name." She takes the baby back from me.

I leave.

Sami's outside, waiting for me.

"Augur named her Jenifer," I say, sitting down next to her. "Summer wanted her to be Ella." I try to keep the venom out of my voice.

"That sucks," Sami says. She's never fooled.

"Yeah." I still have the taste of vomit in my mouth. "It does."

Now

I'm not entirely sure how I wound up in this office, but here I am.

The man across the desk introduced himself as Dr. Yen. The wall behind him is lined with certificates. A single, giant, purple flower blooms from a clay pot on a small table in the corner.

I remember Augur's views on therapy clear as day. One sermon where he said that therapists and doctors were playing God. Another where he said therapy was selfish because it meant you were blaming your problems on other people and de-centering God. Those are my beliefs too. I won't forget that.

I'm too strong.

Really the only reason I'm here is because the Tired Man said if I didn't agree to go, he'd send me to a psychiatric ward.

I can't forget that either.

Dr. Yen clears his throat.

"How are you doing today, Gracelyn?" He adjusts the line of pencils on his desk.

What does he expect me to say?

He doesn't seem terribly fazed by my silence. "I need to get one thing out of the way," he says. "Some information I need you to clarify. Is that something you can do for me?"

This time he takes my silence for approval and starts to read from a piece of paper in front of him. "Is your name Gracelyn Cathrine Joan Alvereb-Green?"

I nod. There's no point in lying, he already kind of knows.

"How old are you?"

"Fifteen."

He smiles at my breach of silence. "Okay. Great. That's quite a name. Do you have any nicknames?"

"Some of my friends called me Gracie."

"May I call you that?"

"No."

"Okay, then whatever you're most comfortable with." He's much too cheerful. "Before we start, I always like to tell my patients a little bit about myself, since I'll be getting to know so much about you. Does that sound good?"

I shrug. He gets very excited at that.

"Well, my name is John Yen. I was born in Edison, New Jersey, in nineteen-eighty-two. I like pizza, dogs, and classical music—especially Brahms. I lived in Chicago for a while after medical school but came back here when I got married. My wife and I are expecting our first child in three months."

He looks so genuinely excited to be telling me about his life that I almost feel bad about what I say next. Almost.

"Dr. Yen, I know the truth. I know that you're a disbeliever appointed by the government to divert me from my true calling."

"And what calling is that?" he asks, looking vaguely amused.

"God's calling." *Obviously.*

"Can I ask you a question?"

I nod.

"If all that's true, why did you come here today?"

"Because the Tired Man told me that if I didn't, I'd have to go to a mental facility."

"Who?"

"The Tired Man, the one who brought me here."

"Nathan Spicer?"

"If you like."

The corner of his mouth lifts just a bit, and he scribbles something down on the notepad in front of him. "Why do you call him 'the Tired Man' if you know his name?"

"I mean, do I have to call him Nathan?"

"No. But I'd say it's a bit impolite. What's wrong with a mental facility?"

Is he kidding? I stay silent, and he spends a solid minute writing in his notepad.

"I've asked you quite a few questions, Gracelyn. Do you want to ask me any?"

I shift in my seat a bit. "Do you believe in the afterlife?"

He looks startled. I don't think this was the kind of question he was expecting. "You know, I'm not sure." He thinks for a moment. "I try to believe only what I can see, but I like to hope there's something out there, because I don't like to believe this is all for nothing."

He's a logical man who gives logical answers. It's the wrong answer, of course, but I like it just the same.

"I have another question," I say. "Do *you* know what happened that day?"

There's a moment of uncomfortable silence, because we both know what I'm talking about.

He clears his throat. "Yes. Do you?"

I probably hesitate a moment too long, because he nods in sympathy.

"If you wanted me to, I could tell you exactly what happened that day. I have the full report in my drawer. But I would need you to talk to me. I need us to be able to communicate and be honest. You've been through so much, Gracelyn. Before I tell you what I know, I need to know that you're able to handle it."

I don't answer for a moment.

"I'll take my chances with the news," I say.

We spend the rest of the session in silence.

"So, how was it?" the Tired Man asks Dr. Yen when we walk out of his office and into the soothing beige-colored lobby.

"Gracelyn is very responsive. We have a lot of work to do, but I think she's going to grow a lot with the right treatment. And the right doctor, of course." He and the Tired Man laugh. "All right, see you next week, Nathan. And you too, Gracelyn."

Outside, as he opens the passenger's side door for me, the Tired Man turns and waves again at Dr. Yen, who is barely visible through the building's glass doors. I use my good foot to get into the car, and then I pull up my other leg before shutting the door.

"How do *you* think it went?" the Tired Man asks, slipping into the driver's seat and motioning for me to put on my seatbelt.

I think hard about my answer as we drive off. "I think he's nice... for a disbeliever. I mean, he's being employed by the government, so I don't really trust him. Still, he seems like he cares about his family, and about his job, so I guess it went okay."

The Tired Man just looks at me, baffled.

"Oh, Gracelyn," he says, slowing down for a red light, "what am I going to do with you?"

Two Years Before

I t's my birthday today.

I share a birthday week with a few other people, so usually we have a little party, but I don't know if it'll happen this year. Augur has been in a bad mood, so if we do have a party, we'll have to keep it down and not disturb him.

Sami wakes me up this morning way earlier than we're supposed to be up. She turned twelve a few months ago, and every year for as long as I can remember, I've drawn something for her, and she's written me a poem. This year? Nothing. Well, nothing from her.

"I tried," she apologizes. "They were all crap."

"It's okay." I'm a little disappointed though. I've stashed all her poems in my pillowcase. I was excited to add another.

She hops down from the bunk and heads toward the door. "Come on," she whispers. "You didn't think that I completely forgot about getting you a present, did you?" I follow, being careful not to make any noise. It's still dark outside. Sami climbs up the stairs ahead of me, stepping around the creaky floorboards. I'm not so careful, and she nearly jumps out her skin every time I take a step. "Sheesh, keep it down, willya?"

I stick out my tongue at her.

On the top floor, we head toward the big window at the end of the hallway.

Sami opens the window and steps out. I've never put together that the window would open onto our roof, but clearly Sami has. I'm nervous. I don't like heights. "Come on, dummy," she coaxes.

Clenching my teeth, I climb through the window and place my feet shakily on the slanted roof. Sami just sits there, grinning. I plop down next to her and press my feet firmly on the slanting shingles in front of me. "So, what's the deal? What are we doing out here?"

"Just wait a bit," she says.

"Why have we never done this before?"

"I come up here all the time."

"What?"

"Yeah," she pats the roof like it's some kind of dog. "I mean, I'll probably stop now that you know about it."

"Why? I'm not coming up here without you, don't worry."

"It's just more fun when it's a secret."

"Well, it can be *our* secret."

She smiles at me, but I get the feeling that this is a one-time thing. I get it. We all need something for ourselves.

"I still don't know what my present is," I say after a moment.

"Patience. You'll find out soon." She leans back and looks up at the fading stars in the sky.

Last night, I was crying, and she climbed into bed with me. She wrapped her arms around my back and held me close to her, so tightly I barely had enough breath to keep crying with.

We never talk about when she does that, even though sometimes I want to thank her. I also want to tell her I was crying about how Summer forgot my birthday, because she's so busy with Jenifer. But then I'd have to bring it up, and I'm pretty sure we'd both be embarrassed.

"You ever feel like you don't want to grow up?" I say after a moment.

"We don't have to. We'll just stay up here. There's not enough gravity to stretch out your limbs." She smiles at me. "We can stay like this forever if we want."

"That sounds nice."

"We wouldn't have to deal with anything if we don't want to. No sermons. No work. No...him."

Him. No one ever says anything negative about him. It's not a written rule, but it might as well be. But Sami is outspoken. Impulsive. Annoying at times. She gets mad, throws tantrums, says what she thinks. Aunt Elizabeth always says, "Someone ought to put that girl in her place."

Summer once asked me if I wanted to make different friends. "You don't *have* to hang out with her all the time." But I don't see why I need a new friend. Sami gets me, and I don't think I would like half the stuff we do here as much without her. Sure, she's a little bit temperamental and possessive, but she's my best friend. She's always been there for me.

"What about him?"

"Just... doing confessions, the punishments, and feeling like—" She sits up suddenly. "Gracie, look!"

A beautiful sunrise has turned the whole sky pink. Me, Sami, and the roof are bathed in orange light. "Wow."

"Happy Birthday."

I lean into her. No words necessary.

But just as I do, the shingle under my foot breaks away from the roof, and I lose my balance, sliding all the way down to the edge, only stopping myself with the pressure of my feet and by digging my fingernails into the soft textured wood.

"Fuck!" Sami scrambles down and grabs my arm. "Fuck!"

I've never heard her swear before. In fact, I don't think I've ever heard anyone swear, other than Uncle Hiram. She probably learned it from him.

My forearms are burning, and my feet are inches above the lip of the roof and starting to slide. "Help, Sami!"

"What the hell does it look like I'm trying to do?" she hisses. I would laugh if I weren't about to die.

Augur never lets us go off the compound, even for medical care. A few years ago, one of Aunt Jane's sons, Abel, got tangled up in the barbed wire part of our fence. Despite all Aunt Reina's efforts, he died from an infection. I don't want to fall off this roof and be dead by the end of the week because of a broken ankle.

Sami is trying to hold on to me by my arm, but she's smaller than me, and she's losing the battle.

I hear stirring inside the house. Not surprising considering the amount of noise we're making.

"Come on, Gracie, just hold on," says Sami.

I'm looking up at her, and I can see people above us, leaning out the window. I relax for a moment, thinking I'm going to be saved, but that's all it takes for me to lose my grip on Sami and for her to lose her grip on me. Screaming, I slip over the edge of the roof and plummet to the ground below.

Now

The Tired Man has finally given in. He's agreed to let me watch the news.

It's clear to me I've been getting too comfortable in his home, getting seduced by pizza and movies and Lauren being nice to me. I'm losing my way. Maybe the watching the news will shake me up and force me to remember things, give me the fortitude to do what I need to do.

I've been waiting days for this chance. Apparently, most stations have moved on, but the Tired Man says there's a "Sixty Minutes" special on tonight.

Lauren says she'll keep an eye on me, to make sure that I don't lose my mind. Honestly, I don't blame the Tired Man for being worried about that. It's possible he's right to be.

I just don't know yet.

As I settle into the couch, across from the television, a lump forms in my throat. *What if they show the bodies?* Lauren puts her feet up on the coffee table, and I see the writing on the top of her socks. "Nevertheless, she persisted."

I don't think I'm ready to see bodies. I don't know if I'm ready for any of this.

I've bitten my fingernails down to almost nothing. The cuticles are red and inflamed.

Lauren flips through channels. I see brief flashes of things I haven't watched in years: a cartoon featuring a family with yellow skin; a football game. She finally stops flipping when we arrive on a woman wearing a man's suit, looking directly into the camera. It's feels like she's looking right at me.

"It's been over a month since the tragedy at the compound of the Holy Savior's Church doomsday cult in Garrisfield, California..." she says.

My breath catches in my throat.

"...and the controversy surrounding government actions has only grown more heated. Protestors and lawyers say the ATF handled the case poorly—going in unannounced, not following proper procedures. The leader of the group, Randolph Milly, was trapped inside the burning compound during the standoff and died from smoke inhalation. Had he survived, it's likely he would have spent the rest of his life in prison for child abuse, polygamy, and first-degree murder. In all, nine government agents and one hundred and fourteen members of Milly's congregation died, some apparently from gunshot wounds they could not possibly have inflicted on themselves." She pauses dramatically, taking a deep breath. "There is also speculation that the fire was not the result of the government firing tear gas, but was, in fact, set by Milly or his followers..."

Over her voice, images appear on the screen. An overhead picture of our home on fire, and then a still photo of Augur preaching to us. It's an old picture from the false alarm. I've seen it before. Some of our faces are blurred out—I guess those of us who are still alive. I can see Uncle Dan in the front row of our little chapel. Augur has his arms spread wide. My chest tightens.

The woman's face comes back on-screen. "Perhaps most disturbing of all," she says, "are the crimes committed by members of the church before any of this even happened. The reason that the government agents were there in the first place, to arrest four members who—"

Lauren picks up the remote and switches off the TV.

I realize that I'm crying. It hurts to breathe.

"I think that's enough for tonight, yeah?" Lauren says hurriedly, glancing back and forth between me and the TV screen, as if it might turn back on without her permission. "Maybe go to sleep? Or have some ice cream?" Her hand is hovering next to my head, as if she wants to put it on my back to comfort me.

"What kind of ice cream?" I ask, wiping my nose with the back of my sleeve.

"We've only got vanilla."

"Vanilla's good."

When she comes back, it's with two bowls heaped with melty, creamy blobs of white. I eat mine as slowly as I can because the more time I spend eating it, the more time Lauren will babble about her school, and the longer she does that, the longer I can pretend that my life isn't what she would probably call a big hot mess.

"Nathan says you and his daughter get along very well," Dr. Yen says. I'm watching the Newton's Cradle on his desk swing back and forth, remembering the one Aunt Salma gave to Augur as a wedding gift. "Gracelyn?"

I look at him. "Lauren is nice to me. And she trusts me. Unlike some people."

"Do you think Nathan doesn't trust you?" he asks, scribbling on the notepad.

I nod. "But you know, I'm not sure he should."

"Why wouldn't he?" he says, looking a little worried.

He believes people are good. He wants to believe that I can be fixed, that nothing about my soul is tainted, that I'm young enough to be saved.

So, I decide to tell him something.

"In the toilet tank in the bathroom by my room, there's a removable piece called a trip lever. I could use it to cut his carotid artery, or mine, or Lauren's, or all of ours, and we'd bleed out before anyone could stop it. Or I could turn my bedsheets into a rope and hang myself or strangle someone. I know where every pressure point on a child, man or woman is located. I could kill you right now if I wanted to, in ten different ways. He shouldn't trust me. You shouldn't. No one should."

I stop talking and gleefully watch his face as the corner of his mouth twitches and his serious doctor expression slips ever so slightly.

"Well, Gracelyn, I'm not sure what to say about all that," he says. He thinks about it for a moment. "I guess what I wonder is if you *want* to do those things. Would you ever want to hurt Lauren, who you say trusts you? Or Nathan, who, whether or not you care, has been protecting you since you arrived. I wonder if you could ever actually harm me."

Of course, I could. Augur always said that if we had to hurt or even kill disbelievers, we should. That's why he taught us how to shoot a gun. That's why he gave us anatomy lessons. But when I try to imagine snapping Lauren's neck, I feel sick.

"Gracelyn," he says, responding to my silence. "Just because they raised you to be a weapon doesn't mean you have to be used that way."

It makes me mad that what I just said doesn't seem to bother him more, that he remains so calm.

"Have you spoken to any of the other children yet?" he asks, pivoting suddenly.

I shake my head.

"Why not?"

"Because..." I don't have an answer. My heart aches to hear Jenifer's tiny voice. I wish I could talk to Fawn. "Something about talking with them feels like it's too..."

"Much?" he suggests.

"Yes. Too much."

"I'm sure they'd love to talk to you. Who do you want to speak to the most?"

I hesitate. I know the answer. I just don't want to tell him.

He scribbles something down. "When are you allowed to talk to them?"

"On Saturdays at three-thirty."

"Well, you know, our meeting ends at two. Maybe you could talk to them today."

Maybe I could.

Two Years Before

Aunt Reina says I should have broken both my legs.

"*Y*ou fell off a roof!" *s*he keeps saying, tsking at me and adding, "You are a very stupid, lucky girl."

I don't feel very lucky. My left knee has no skin on it, and there's a massive bump on the back of my head. Sami's come to visit me in the medical room quite a few times in the past few days, feeling very guilty, though that hasn't stopped her from cracking jokes. As of this morning, I'm back in my own bed. I've heard several people say that I'm being lazy since I haven't moved all day. I'm too tired to care.

In the middle of the night, something wakes me up. When I open my eyes, Sami is right in front of my face. Before I can yelp, she claps her hand over my mouth. My first instinct is to lick her hand like a little kid, but I don't get the chance because she takes her hand away and whispers, "Sorry. I just didn't want you to wake anyone up."

I'm still half asleep and confused.

"Augur wants to see us," she hisses.

My heart races, partly from excitement, partly from fear. It's the dead of night. What could he possibly want?

"Okay," I say.

Sami grabs my hand, and we tiptoe down the hall.

"What do you think he wants?"

She shrugs. "He just asked, at dinner. Said to wait until it was dark."

We inch the doors open and move as quietly as we can towards the chapel. I put my arm over her shoulders and she helps me walk forward. "It's kind of weird that he wants to see us at night, right?"

"He's busy during the day," she says. Even though it's hot and dusty all year long, nights in the desert are cold. I'm shivering.

"Yeah, but he doesn't usually allow us to break curfew." We climb the chapel steps, and Sami knocks on the door.

Augur opens the door a crack, blinding us with his smile. "Hello girls," he says. "Come inside. I can't have you freezing out here."

Sami leads the way, always so much braver than me.

The chapel never ceases to amaze me. In our bedrooms, kitchen and bathrooms, everything is shabby, old, stained, and grimy. But in the chapel, the carpet gets vacuumed almost every day, and every pew is polished. I remember the week we spent making the stained-glass windows when I was six. The simple designs and bright colors make the whole room bright and beautiful during the day. Candles and hanging lamps light the building at night.

"I'm guessing you two are a little confused." We both nod, still shivering slightly. "But God has spoken to me, and he does not make mistakes." Augur motions for us to sit down in the first row of pews. "He has told me I alone should not carry the gift of music. I need to pass my knowledge on to the younger members of our church. One day, your job will be to soothe your own children with this gift."

He walks over to the lectern and pulls out an acoustic guitar from behind it.

My heart beats faster. "Do we get to play it?" I ask.

He laughs a little and walks back toward us. "Yes, Gracelyn, you do." He holds the guitar out to me. "I thought you might be excited about this. Consider it a late birthday present." There's a glint in his eye.

I look over at Sami, who doesn't seem quite as excited (though she does smile at me). *Go ahead.* I reach out and take the instrument from him.

I've seen Augur play the electric guitar many times, and the acoustic guitar a few times. He says that before he found God, he wanted to be a rock star. I think he could have been. Whenever he plays, even if I'm dancing or singing, I watch him. Not him, actually, but what he's doing, the way he handles the instrument.

"We'll start with a few chords. Then maybe I'll teach you a short song. But once the sun rises, you'll have to learn the rest on your own." Augur sits cross-legged on the raised stage area underneath the lectern. He pats a spot next to him and I run to sit in it. I hold the guitar the way I've seen him hold it, letting him place my fingers on the strings. "This is a C-chord."

Sami sits and watches us from a nearby pew.

Augur shows me five different chords. Every time I play one correctly, I feel a flutter of excitement. Even just hearing the word "good" from him makes me want to jump up and down. I've never had his full attention like this. I'm so caught up in what we're doing that after a while I forget Sami's even in the chapel with us. When I finally remember and look over, I see she's asleep, curled up on the hardwood bench.

"All right, Gracelyn," Auger says. "It's time to teach you a song." Outside, through the window, the first hints of approaching morning lighten the sky. "How about *Amazing Grace*?" He cracks a smile at his own pun.

I nod furiously.

He lays out the sheet music in front of me. It takes longer to learn a song than it did to learn the chords. By the time I can awkwardly play it all the way through, the sun has come up. Augur looks at me proudly, smiling, laughing off my mistakes. I'm glowing inside. This is literally the best day of my life.

When I finish playing *Amazing Grace* for the third time, Augur stands up and claps. "Gracelyn, you have a God-given gift. I see great potential in you."

"Thank you, Augur." I try to hand the guitar and sheet music back to him, but he refuses to take them. In fact, he goes and gets more sheet music and adds it to the stack I hold.

"All of this belongs to you now. I won't always be able to play for our family. Maybe one day you'll take my spot in the band. Learn these songs by heart. Maybe one day you'll play them for everyone."

I flush, feeling the warm flutter again.

"All right now, let's go get some sleep before breakfast," he says. We wake Sami, and she groggily makes her way with us to the door. Outside, Augur holds Sami back and whispers something in her ear.

"What did he say to you?" I ask when she catches up to me.

"It's not important," she says, holding my gaze. "Does it feel good to be his favorite?"

The glow inside me dims. "Sami, I—" I reach out, putting my hand on her arm, but she pulls away, leaving me to limp back alone.

Now

I've never used a phone before. There was one landline at home, but I never used it. I had no one to call.

The Tired Man's phone isn't pretty like Lauren's. His is black and heavy with a clear case. He had to make a few calls before he could even reach the people I want to talk to, and when he hands me the phone, it's a bit warm. My hands are so sweaty that I nearly drop it.

"Okay, you have forty-five minutes, but it seems like there are a lot of people who want to talk to you." He smiles.

I press the phone to my ear and hear a woman's voice. She's not talking directly to me, she's talking to someone nearby, in the kind of baby voice Augur would get upset about parents using.

"Do you want to talk to her?"

I hear some noise, no words, just faint voices. "Okay, here you go. It's on speaker, but don't everyone talk at once. Don't overwhelm her."

Ten voices chime in at once. I hear my name a few times, and Fawn's telling everyone to be quiet, to go one at a time. Just the sound of her voice makes tears spring to my eyes. Everyone goes quiet. Fawn asks: "Can you hear us, Gracie?"

I do my best to not let them know I'm crying. "Yeah," I manage. "I can hear."

"Aw, she's crying!" says someone. I'm not sure if it's Yotam or his brother, Abraham.

"Be quiet, Yotam, she's just emotional," says Fawn. *Right*, I remember. *Abraham is dead.* "Okay, everyone get in line, I want to talk to her." I hear moving and shuffling. "Gracie? Where are you? They won't tell us."

I try to pull myself together. "I'm in this place New Jersey. It's all the way across the country. I think my clock is even three hours ahead of yours." *Well, don't make it sound too cool.*

"Are you okay?" Fawn's tone is so soothing and loving, I can't bear to let her know the truth, that I'm nowhere near okay. I want to be there with her and all the other kids. I miss them so much.

"I'm with a man called Nathan and his daughter. They seem nice. His daughter is only a bit younger than me."

"We all wish you were here."

I stay silent, doing my best not to cry again.

"Do you want to talk to Jenifer?"

"Yeah, can I?"

"Grathie!" says Jenifer's tiny two-year-old voice. My name doesn't even sound like a word. "I miss you!"

"I miss you too, Jenifer. Are you doing good today?" I feel like a baby myself, unable to control my emotions.

"Yeah! I got a popfickle!" I hear soft laughter coming from everyone else.

Hearing their voices brings a huge smile to my face. It also reminds me of all the ones that are missing.

Eve and Dawn, the twins, are both excited about their situation, as they get to draw all the time, and they love the food there. I think they'll be okay. Their father, Uncle Jim, is alive.

Kyle is the oldest kid there, but he's always been quiet, so he doesn't offer much more than a hello. Still, it makes me happy to hear his voice. He tells me that they saw Juniper for a bit before someone came for her, and he's sure she would have wanted to talk to me if she were there.

Besides ordering everyone around, Fawn tells me about her therapist, who pops cherry cough drops nonstop during their meetings. Fawn is the third oldest left alive, sixteen (almost seventeen), and she's clearly in charge of them. She tells me that the littlest kids have been having nightmares after I try to ask strategic questions, to figure out what they're doing there, without freaking her out.

Vera refuses to show any kind of emotion, even though everyone else's voice has a hint of fear or worry in it. She tells me she has an awesome nurse who helped her with the bullet wound in her leg.

Yotam and Michel tease me like always, knowing I can't give them playful smacks on the arm. Nelly, who always wanted to be one of the boys, tries to join in, and to my surprise, the boys let her.

Edward is pretty young and was always really quiet, but Thomas, who's about the same age, chatters away like Aunt Glinda.

After each of them has a turn talking with me, it seems like they go back to playing or drawing or reading. Wherever they are, it seems they have lots of entertainment.

And then, when the forty-five minutes is almost over, Sami gets on the phone.

"Hi."

"Hi." I try to sound as calm as I can.

"How are you?" she asks, sounding unsure of herself.

"I'm okay." I pause. "What about you?"

"Well, I hate going to therapy, but the food's good."

"Why wouldn't you like talking about your life? It's not like you have anything to hide."

Shit, I shouldn't have said that.

"You haven't..." Sami starts. "You haven't told anyone about..."

"No, and you better not either."

In the background, I hear the woman's voice say, "All right kiddos, time's up." There are a few *aws* from the younger kids, and the sounds of movement, shuffling of feet. The woman's voice gets louder. She says, "Thank you for talking to everyone. It was the highlight of their day, really. If you want to talk to them again next week, I'm sure they would love that." Like they're dogs being given treats.

"I might," I say. "Thank you." And then I press the red end-call button. I put the phone down, gulping air and sobbing, my chest practically convulsing.

I've cried here before, more times than I can count, but I truly believe that nothing could be worse than this pain, this guilt. These children's families are dead. So many other children are dead. It's so unfair. Summer is gone, and Jenifer needs her. I deserved to die much more than she did. Why was I the one spared?

The Tired Man comes in, probably hearing me crying from the kitchen. I know he's been listening.

He kneels down next to the chair I'm in, reaches out. "Gracelyn? Are you all right?"

I whack his hand away so hard it hurts. "No, I'm not all right! How could you possibly look at me and think I'm all right? Just get away from me! I hate you! I hate you! I hate you!"

Three Months Before

Practice is crucial, that's what Augur always says. You should practice everything you do as much as you can, and shooting is no exception.

Sami and I are finally old enough to join the adults in target practice. For years, we were only allowed to watch, but now we even have our own guns assigned to us. "A Colt 1911," Uncle Liam crooned, "Good for beginners, but it's no joke." It's heavy and cold in my hand.

After Augur gives his speech about the disbelievers and the need to protect ourselves, we start shooting. I'm nervous. I've always hated the sound of a gun. It's loud and sudden, but after a few shots, I get used to it. I'm hitting the center of the target with ease.

Uncle Hiram, who's watching over the youngest kids, puts a hand on my shoulder, and says loudly, "Look here, everybody, we've got quite the young marksman." I beam as people come over to inspect my handiwork and pat me on the back. I see Sami out of the corner of my eye. She's staring at me, and the look on her face makes my grin disappear.

After practice, Sami and I walk over to the porch and sit in the shade on the steps. Uncle Dan says it must be over a hundred degrees today. Fanning myself, I can feel Sami's eyes on me.

"What?" I snap.

"Nothing," she says, "Want me to braid your hair?"

I hold up my wrist, where there are two hair ties. She grabs the first one and places it between her teeth as she takes hold of my hair.

"Why were you looking at me like that during target practice?"

"I wasn't looking at you like anything." She removes the hair tie from her mouth and twists it around the end of the first braid. I put up my wrist again, and she takes the other tie.

"You were. I saw you."

"You're imagining things." She ties off the second braid, brushing her fingers against my neck.

"Am not." I whirl around to face her.

With her curls pulled back, I can see her entire face. "Are too," she says.

We're so close to each other that I can see a drop of sweat sliding down her forehead. Something about Sami's face reminds me of an angel. Her brown skin is smooth and her eyes are big like the eyes of the cherubs on our stained-glass windows.

I pull away from her, rocking back on my heels. "Maybe I am imagining things."

"No, I—" She wipes the sweat away. "Look, I'm just jealous, okay? You're already good at shooting, and I suck."

I can't help but grin. "Yeah, you do."

She laughs and shoves me lightly. I throw my arm over her shoulder, even though it's way too hot to do so. "Come on, Uncle Dan might have some popsicles for us."

Now

M y cast is off.

I had one more x-ray, and Dr. Keller asked what I would rate my pain on a scale of one to ten. I rated it a two. She got excited, and my gamble in not saying a one, paid off. She removed the cast. When she started up the saw, I recoiled, but despite the loud whining buzz, it didn't hurt, it just tickled. Not that I allowed myself to laugh.

Sitting on the bed now, I can't help but stare in disgust at my foot. It looks weird: red, sweaty, dirty and flakey. But that doesn't matter. The cast is off. That means that in less than a month, I'll be able to walk properly. I'll be able to run.

The moment the Tired Man leaves my lunch on the bedside table and closes the door behind him, I attempt to walk across the room. Once my foot starts to ache, I stop. I may be desperate, but I'm not stupid. While resting on the desk chair, I notice the yellow bus as it pulls up to the curb just like it does every day at 3:10. But this time, two other kids get off with Lauren. I've never seen them before, not even on days when I can see through the windows of the bus.

The girl reminds me of Fawn. She has thick dark hair, long and braided the way Fawn liked hers.

The boy looks like he could be Lauren's darker-haired twin. He wears thick black glasses and a sweatshirt much too light for this weather. All three of them wear what I assume is their school uniform under their jackets. Clean white polo shirts, wrinkled to varying degrees. Lauren and the other girl wear dark blue gingham skirts.

That's what they do in outside schools. They force you to be the same as everyone else.

I really want to know what they're saying. It feels sneaky. I mean, it's not like I owe Lauren any real loyalty, it's just that I don't want to ruin things between us. I like having someone to talk to.

But once they get upstairs, it's impossible *not* to listen. The walls are thin, and they're all talking loudly. I hop quietly across the room and slump down on the bed. Leaning against the wall, I can hear everything they're saying.

"Do you guys want some food or anything?" Lauren asks.

"I don't know. Do you guys *have* food or anything?" The boy.

"Shut up, George." That's the girl.

"What? I'm just saying, outside of school, no one's seen you or your dad in a month. Not even at the supermarket."

Silence. I guess that's a subject no one was going to bring up.

"Sorry, I'll stop talking now."

"No, no, it's okay. You're right. We've been hibernating."

"Do you want to talk about it?" This comes from the girl, again.

"Um." Lauren. There's a long pause. "Well. She's living with us, in the room across the hall. She's sort of calmed down. She talks to people now at least—well, to me. I think she's said a few words to my dad just to be polite or something, but other than that, I think she kinda hates him." She laughs hollowly. "She's going to the same therapist as your brother, Vi."

"Dr. Yen? Huh. Well, Zack says he's nice." The girl—Vi—says this.

"What, like, happened to her?" says George. "I mean, is she hurt? Did anyone try to..." He gets quieter, but I can still hear him. "Kill her?"

"She has a broken foot, but that happened afterwards. She has these scars on her arms. I don't know. Her sister was *married* to that guy who died."

"She was married to the leader?"

A chill goes down my spine.

"Yeah. Like, when she was fifteen."

"How do you even become a cult leader?" Vi asks. "Like, how does that happen?"

"Well, Ray, if someone asks you if you're a God, you say yes." *Who is Ray?* They must all know, because they laugh.

"I wish I hadn't watched the news," Lauren says once the laughter dies. "I get really nervous that she's going to, like, kill herself during the night. Sometimes—I hope this doesn't sound too weird—I go in her room and watch her sleep. I read about how they had suicide classes, shooting practice, and wrestling. She looks really frail, but apparently she could murder me in, like, forty different ways...She talks in her sleep, too."

"Your dad said it was okay for us to come over, though?" George says.

"Well, not exactly." I hear the sheepishness in Lauren's voice. "But he feels bad that I haven't done anything fun since she got here, so he won't get mad, at least not in front of you guys. He might make asparagus later, though, just to watch me suffer." They all laugh at this. "But I'm fine. Let's to my original question—either of you hungry?" I hear them walk down the hall, down the stairs.

I sit on the bed, my knees pulled up to my chin. Outsiders are so callous. They change the subject in a blink. Forgive each other with the snap of a finger. They're so jaded to other people's suffering.

I'm still sitting there, feeling sorry for myself, when there's a knock on the door.

I open it to find Lauren standing in front of me, wearing a guilty smile, holding the same package of sandwich cookies as always. "I know I'm late, but here." She puts them on the side table, then sits on the end of the bed. To my shock and horror, Vi and George appear in the doorway, and sort of cautiously take a few steps into the room.

"Nice to meet you. You're Gracelyn, right?" Vi says. She takes a tentative seat on the edge of the armchair, as far away from me as possible. "I'm Violet."

"So I heard," I say, taking a cookie.

Violet looks incredibly uncomfortable. By contrast, George doesn't seem fazed at all. He drops his backpack on the floor and flops down next to it. "Well then, you must know my name," he says. "Tybalt Nottingham the third..."

"Shut up," says Violet, smacking his shoulder in a playful, almost flirty way. "He's George Byrnes the first, and a complete idiot."

"You should talk," George says.

"Oh my God, you two, get a room," says Lauren, rolling her eyes. They both go crimson.

"Maybe you and Alex should," Violet says pointedly.

Now Lauren goes red. "Okay, let's change the subject. Maybe Gracelyn wants to hear about what our day at school was like since she's never been." She looks at me hopefully.

"You mean like Mr. Dallasandro?" George says.

"Oh my God, Mr. Dallasandro! What a complete and total dick. He gave me a C-minus for my history project and now my class grade is like two points lower."

"You need to calm down Vi, you're gonna be fine," says George, chewing on an energy bar excavated from the depths of his backpack.

"Tell that to my grandparents," Violet grumbles.

"Why? They aren't in charge of you."

"I feel bad, though. My parents don't care, but if one more of the grandchildren doesn't go to college, Nana says she'll have a heart attack."

"So you'll go to art school instead, right? You'll be amazing there," says Lauren.

"Well, when she says college, she means for business or something," Vi says with a sigh.

"Well, fuck them," says George. "Who wants to go to business school? You'll be a great artist, and they'll be sorry."

Violet blushes so hard I think her face might erupt. "Thanks, George."

Lauren gives me a look as if apologizing for her friends.

I smile a little, strangely grateful to be included.

More stories about school follow. They seem excited to have a fresh audience, even an audience that doesn't respond.

"I wish the musical this year wasn't stupid," says Lauren, finding a ball under the bed which she tosses at George. He catches it and passes it back and forth between his hands.

"Hey, hey. *High School Musical* is not stupid. I'm sorry we're not doing one of your depressing ones," says Violet.

All three of them laugh.

"What's *High School Musical*?" I immediately regret asking when Violet launches into a long monologue, explaining its ridiculous plot, complete with musical interludes of songs they all know. Apparently, Lauren is playing the villain of the show, which everyone seems to agree is because she just dyed her hair pink. George is an ensemble member, and Violet is playing an eccentric teacher.

It's nice to hear what life is like here. I understand so little of what they're talking about, but it's interesting, anyway.

The world is so much bigger than I thought, and even though I know I shouldn't, I'm starting to like watching it expand.

Three Months Before

Every other Saturday, Uncle Dan goes into the nearby town to retrieve our mail and pick up our food.

Augur never leaves, not since the false alarm, and therefore, no one else can leave either, except Uncle Dan. I'm glad it's Uncle Dan who goes, because he often brings back treats. Not many people here would think to do that.

Sometimes he brings a bag of candy for us to split up amongst ourselves, or doughnuts in a pink-and-white box. But today there's nothing sweet for us, just a giant bag of popcorn. The rules are that everyone gets a bowl, and Uncle Dan scoops until there's none left. Sami gets barely any, so I put some of mine in her bowl.

When we go to sit on the porch, people are coming and going with groceries and packages, and we inch away from the stairs.

Sami puts a handful of popcorn into her mouth, and I look down, examining my boots. They're falling apart, the rubber bottoms peeling away at the toes. I might need a new pair. But new things, even new used things, have been harder to come by lately. I'm wearing some of Aunt Holly's pants from when she first joined our group, and they're so old the seams are unraveling. I thought maybe there would be a bag of clothes in the back of the car today, but I was wrong.

What Uncle Dan did bring back is kind of sad. Only enough food to last us two weeks, and that's only if we skip lunch and have oatmeal every morning. This popcorn is the first proper snack we've had in weeks.

Sami nudges me, and I snap out of my spiral of worries. "You gonna eat that?" She motions at my untouched bowl. I realize I haven't eaten any yet and take a handful. "Those pants are falling apart," she says, as if reading my mind. "And it's too hot for them, anyway. Let's get changed." I nod and toss the last kernel of popcorn in my mouth.

The main building has two sleeping quarters on the first floor. The men's quarters are on the left side, the children's on the right, with girls and boys separated by a shower curtain repurposed into a barrier. Between them is the kitchen and living area, as well as four long tables, which can somehow seat our entire congregation at once. The second floor is where Augur and the women have their quarters.

Sami and I still live with the children. But when we marry Augur or get to be eighteen, we'll move to the women's quarters. Whichever comes first.

There aren't any private rooms in the main house other than the bathrooms, and those are barely big enough for one person at a time. Despite that, Sami and I grab some lighter clothes and squeeze into the tiny children's bathroom.

I sit down in the bathtub to make room for Sami to get changed. I look at the wall instead of her, though I can see her arms flailing around out of the corner of my eye.

"What are you looking at?" she asks suddenly. "What's so interesting about that moldy wall?"

"Nothing," I say, turning to look at her.

There almost aren't words for how pretty Sami is. Even in this tiny, windowless bathroom, her hair and skin glow. She has the kind of face that makes you think of perfect, sunshiney days.

I look away from her again, self-conscious about staring.

"Oh, I get it," she says. "My beauty is just too overwhelming for you."

Now I *have* to look at her, though I make a show of twisting my face in disgust. "I hate you."

"Nah," she says, "You love me."

I blush so hard I'm sure she can feel the heat from where she is.

When she's finished changing, I step from the tub and take my turn changing out of my falling-apart pants into a pair of cutoff shorts. Sami gathers our clothes from the tiled floor, and we leave the tiny bathroom together, not making eye contact until we reach the kids' quarters.

I don't know why we're acting so weird. We're friends.

Friends.

I mean, she's beautiful, of course. With her halo of curls, smooth dark skin, and brown eyes that glimmer with mischief. Beautiful.

Anyone who knows her would say it.

Outside, nearly all the family gathers by the gate, watching a car approach in a swirl of dust. We rush out to join them. Excited whispers. Just as the car stops, Sami grabs my hand and squeezes to let me know everything is fine.

There's a couple in the car. The man gives everyone a big smile as he gets out, taking off his bright blue sunglasses. He looks like he's in his mid-thirties. Prematurely gray streaked hair. Handsome, but not in a remarkable way. He strikes me as the type of person who wakes up at five in the morning to go jogging.

"That was quite a drive," the woman exclaims as she closes her door. "Y'all really are in the middle of nowhere!" She reaches out to shake everyone's hand that she can, her enormous brown eyes warm and friendly. She seems a little younger than the man, quite beautiful, though in a way that seems performative, as if she's thought carefully about the image she wants to present. Her blonde hair is held back with a flower clip.

"I'm Gina. This is my husband, Oliver. Nice to meet, y'all."

I've never heard an accent like hers before, but it draws me in. I like it.

A few people in our crowd start murmuring. The couple looks at each other, suddenly uncomfortable. Then everything goes quiet, and Augur parts the crowd, walking towards the newcomers with a neutral expression.

"Hello, folks. I'm Randolph. Pleasure to meet you both. What brings you to our humble home?"

"Well, Randolph, some nice people in that town nearby said what you're doing here is something really special," Oliver says.

Augur smiles. It must be nice to hear that his message is spreading. I know it fuels his ego.

Augur doesn't have an ego. Being egotistical is a sin.

"Summer, Holly, show these nice people around," he says, and heads back to the main house.

I look at Sami. She's as confused as I am.

Now

Lauren's friends leave when the Tired Man calls her for dinner, but she doesn't go downstairs right away.

"Um. Dad said to ask you if you wanted to eat with us tonight."

I blink at her.

"But, you know, if you don't want to, that's totally cool. I know it's a lot in one day."

Don't get too comfortable. Don't.

"What are we having?" I ask. *Stupid.*

"We ordered a bunch of stuff from this takeout place. You can have whatever."

Don't. Don't.

"Sorry, I don't think I will," I say. *Good girl.*

Lauren's face shows a brief flicker of disappointment, but she forces a smile. "It's cool. You don't have to do anything you don't want to."

What I *want* to do is a whole different thing from what I *need* to do.

Because what I really want is to eat something besides soup and crackers. What I want is to take part in their conversations. But what I need to do is stay vigilant. What I need is to be the way Augur taught us to be.

Talking to my family on the phone has opened my eyes. We're all becoming too comfortable.

We haven't done what he trained us to do. At least I haven't. I haven't made another escape attempt. I haven't killed myself. Or them. I haven't even tried.

It's because you like these people. You care about them. You don't want to hurt them.

Alone in my room again, I eat my soup and crackers, plotting my escape. I've been thinking about this since day one, but now it feels tangible. I can taste my freedom. There's one critical issue, which is that there's no way I'm getting out of this house and neighborhood without someone noticing.

Any muscle I had gained over the years from wrestling and gardening is long gone. My foot is healing, but I still need to get some strength back.

If I stretch, I can grab onto the little ledge over the bathroom door and use that to do pullups.

I also resume my pushup routine. Three to begin. Then four, then five. When I get to seven, I collapse on the floor. This is harder than I remember. And my foot is aching already.

Sit-ups come next. Three sets of fifteen to start. Sit-ups are a piece of cake compared to pushups, but I'm still exhausted when I finish.

I begin to formulate a plan.

I'll never make it on the roads. That much is obvious. I need them to lose track of me before I dare to take to a street. But I can't navigate the somewhat-rural area they live in. I can't get directions. So I'll have to start my route somewhere else.

I'm about to do another set of pullups when the Tired Man walks in. He's holding a plate with a sugar cookie on it. The kind Uncle Dan would bring home for our birthdays. The melt-in-your-mouth kind.

"I thought you might want this," he says, placing the plate on the bedside table.

My mouth waters just looking at it. Every impulse in my body screams for me to scarf it down as fast as I can. But I don't. I stand there, one hand still reaching for the ledge.

"I, um, I don't really want you doing that in here," he says. "You could get hurt, and I just don't think it's a good idea..."

If I get hurt, it's part of my training. Rebuilding the earth is not painless work.

To satisfy him, I nod dutifully and sit back on the bed.

He nods thoughtfully, mouths, "Good night," and closes the door.

After he's gone, I do four more finger pushups before climbing into bed.

More therapy. I like the structure my weeks have now. I like having somewhere to go. But I'm coming to loathe the appointments themselves.

"How was the last week?" Dr. Yen asks, tapping his pen on the notebook in front of him. His office is darker than usual; there's a storm raging outside.

"How do you think?" I say. I can do eleven pushups now. I can run short distances. I'm getting closer to where I need to be to make my escape. It's been a great week. But obviously I'm not telling him that.

"Well, based on that response, probably not great." He scribbles something down. "Some of the doctors in California wanted to relay information to you about the other subjects." He peers at me over his glasses. "Do you want to hear it?"

Subjects. That's all we are to these people. They don't care about our well-being or our lives. We're just information vessels that happen to breathe.

"Sure?" my voice tastes bitter.

"Sami has been telling some very interesting stories. You're a big part of them. You two were best friends, correct?"

My heart stops dead in my chest. What has she been telling them? What do they know? How much do they know? Is it about me? About us both?

"She says you were, anyway."

"Yeah, I guess," I say. He looks surprised by my tone.

"Do you want to tell me about that?" he asks.

"Not really."

There's a moment of silence. I look at the door, trying to remember how to get out of the building from here. *Maybe this is how I escape.*

"Is there anything you *do* want to tell me about?"

"No."

He sighs. "I don't have to explain to you, Gracelyn, that this won't work if you don't try."

I shrug. "Maybe I just don't have anything to say."

"Is that because you don't want this to work?"

"No." I play dumb because that's all this is. A dumb game we're playing.

"I've been thinking a lot about what you said the other day. And why you said it. I think I've finally figured it out."

"Really?" I say, amused by his confidence.

"I think you want to scare me away, Gracelyn. I think when someone gets too close, that's what you do. It makes sense. Everyone you ever got close to is dead now, except for Sami." He tilts his head toward me ever so slightly. "Why won't you talk about her?"

It ticks me off that he's come back to this.

"There's nothing to talk about."

"It seems like you were very close."

"You don't know anything about us."

"You're wrong, Gracelyn. I know a great deal."

"So maybe you can tell me whose fault it is that I'm not there with her?"

He falls silent.

"I miss her, I do, but there's just a lot of... stuff going on and I feel—."

His timer goes off, sounding just like it always does, clucking like a chicken. But he ignores it. "You feel what?"

Nice going. "I feel..." And that's when something takes hold of me. My eyes flick to the door. It's nuts, I know that, but I'm not even thinking. I have to get out of here. I jump up off the sofa and make a break for the door.

Three Months Before

Uncle Victor is blind as a bat, so when he's matching up wrestling partners, I always get paired with someone ten times bigger than me, like Uncle Hiram, or someone way too small, like Eve or Dawn, or even tiny Mary.

It's no big surprise when I immediately get paired with new Aunt Gina, who is roughly my size, but so weak and inexperienced I could kill her with one good choke hold. For some reason, though, it feels as if she's letting me win.

"How do you like it here?" I ask when we stop for a water break. She beams at me, showing off the bleeding lip I just gave her.

"I love it. I lived in a big city before this, so it's nice to be out in the fresh air all the time." She speaks in a syrupy, lazy drawl that Aunt Elizabeth says is how everybody down South talks. "You folks really have figured it out."

"What do we have figured out?" I ask, though I'm pretty sure I know what she's going to say.

"How to live. How to get close to Christ. Me and Oliver have spent a long time looking for a place like this." She smiles and swipes at her lip. "But I think I best level up my wrestling game if I want to survive here." She laughs, throwing her head back. I laugh with her. She pulls her hair out of its flower clip and gathers it back up in a neater bun. Being new means she has some style to her hair, it's not just long and untrimmed. I can see dark roots under the blonde.

New people are rare. A lot of people left once the celibacy rule was put in place. Anyone new tends to leave once they learn about it. Same thing with the no hospitals rule. Aunt Reina takes it very personally when people leave because of that.

Aunt Gina seems okay though. The only part she doesn't really like is the last name situation. Gina Green. Which I kinda get. Uncle Oliver hasn't said much to me—or to anyone else for that matter. Aunt Gina is definitely the more sociable one.

"Okay everyone, back here for partners," says Uncle Victor, who is too old to wrestle but not too old to boss everyone around.

He pushes random people together carelessly, not even really looking. Even though he couldn't blow a dandelion off a cliff, his intensity sends Sami slamming into me dramatically.

"Okay, shake hands with your partner, then on my whistle, go."

Sami and I shake hands. Our palms are rough with calluses and damp with sweat.

The whistle blows, and she's already got leverage on my arms. We push each other back and forth across our square of taped-off space, heads almost touching from how hard we're leaning on each other.

Sami is shorter than me, but her arms are bigger, and no matter how hard I push, she still dominates me. It's strength, but it's also technique. She's just better than me.

Once she gets hold of my torso, it's basically all over. Before I can get free, she launches me over her left shoulder, twists me to the floor, and throws her weight on top of me.

Pinning my thigh to the ground with her knee, she lifts one hand in the air, using the other to push down on my chest. "Give up?" she demands. I feel a dribble of blood fall from my nose.

"No," I grunt.

She leans into me even harder, so I can hardly breathe. "How about now?"

"All right, all right." I grunt. "You win."

She loosens her hold. "Sorry, what was that? I couldn't hear you."

"You win, okay? I give up."

She collapses onto me, panting and laughing. "You're heavy. That wasn't easy."

"Shut up," I say, shoving her off me. She stands up, dusts off her clothes, and puts out her hand to help me up. I spring up so quickly that my nose brushes against hers for a moment. "Woah." I didn't mean to say it out loud. She takes a step backward and lets go of my hand.

The whistle blows again, and we all get new partners. My upper lip and chin are smeared with blood. I can taste it, metallic and bitter.

My next partner is frail Uncle Holden. I slam his head so hard into the ground I can feel the vibration in my bones.

"That was weird," says Sami. We're sitting on her bed and she's wiping the dried blood off my face with a damp cloth.

"Was it?"

She puts down the cloth and motions for me to give her a hair tie. "I mean, yeah." She starts doing a French braid with my hair.

"What was weird about it?" I ask, even though I know damn well what was weird about it. She ties off the first braid, somewhat aggressively.

"Come on, Gracie. Don't be thick." She starts on the second one, her fingers moving quickly.

"I'm not. I'm being..." Honestly I don't know what I'm being. She finishes the braid, giving it a harder tug than necessary. "Ow!" I whirl around to face her. "That hurt!"

"Good!" she says.

I'm about to storm off, but her eyes widen, and her face turns from angry to totally petrified.

I hesitate. "Sami, what's wrong?"

She gets up and runs out of the room, pushing past Juniper and Allison, who enter just as she leaves.

"What's—" They look over at me and their faces go white. "Oh, no."

"What? What's going on..." My voice trails off as I see the bright red stain on the sheets where Sami was sitting.

I run after her to the locked bathroom.

"Sami!" I hammer on the door. "Let me in!"

She opens it a crack.

"I-I-I..." She can't even get one word out before she bursts into tears.

I push my way in and lock the door behind me. We're only inches apart in the cramped space. She sobs, falling into my arms. "I don't want—I don't—"

I hold her, feeling her body shudder and shake. "I know," I whisper. "I know."

Everyone knows if Augur finds out you've bled, you become fair game, even if there's no official acknowledgment of that. He can have whomever he wants. All I know is I can't lose Sami.

The thought of it has me crying, too. I want to say something comforting to her, but I can't think of anything.

It would have been nice to never grow up.

There's a soft knock at the door.

"Samira? Gracelyn? I need your help with something upstairs," Aunt Gina drawls from outside. "Could you two come out here?"

I look at Sami and offer her my sleeve to wipe her tears.

"It's weirder if we don't go," I whisper.

"I can say I sat in something."

We offer each other weak smiles and leave.

Aunt Gina takes us upstairs, making small talk and walking behind Sami the whole time. I can see how tense Sami is, but she smiles and nods along with Aunt Gina. She leads us to the biggest of the women's bedrooms, where the unmarried women sleep.

Aunt Elizabeth sits on a bed, her permanent scowl in place. A few other women are around, folding laundry. A few are on their beds, reading the scriptures. The rest must be downstairs, cooking.

Aunt Gina leads us to a back closet and opens it, removing a pink box.

I haven't been up here in a long time. It's the most spartan and least decorated of the quarters. In the kids' quarters, we have strings of lights and drawings the little kids have made. The few times I've been inside the men's quarters, I've seen posters for movies featuring half-naked women and robots. They also have shelves to store what I think are their shaving kits. Honestly, it seems unfair that they get conveniences like that, but they're men. Here, there's hardly anything. A few photographs, curtains on the windows. That's it.

"Now Samira, any time Aunt Flo comes to visit, come to me or Jane." Aunt Gina says. "We'll bring you enough supplies for a few days, and whenever you need more, just ask. And we promise, if you don't want us to, we won't say anything. And only ever use our bathroom, or else someone will find out."

"Wait what? Who's Aunt Flo? What supplies?"

"Oh boy. Uh..." Aunt Gina sits down and motions for us to join her on the floor. "Samira, darling. Do you know what your bleeding means?"

"Sami. Call me Sami." She swallows. "It means I'm ready to have children."

"No, Sami. It means you can get pregnant. It doesn't mean you're ready to have children. You're still a little girl, for crying out loud. But the thing is that if Augur finds out you're having your period and wants to marry you, he can *get* you pregnant. You don't want that, do you?"

Sami hesitates and looks back at me. I don't know if we can trust her either, so I shrug.

Eventually, Sami shakes her head—no she doesn't want that.

"Smart girl," Gina says, smiling.

"Gina, this is blasphemy. There are rules here," interjects Aunt Elizabeth, who has been lurking nearby. "I don't approve of this... thing you and Jane have going on." She tosses one lock of long hair over shoulder.

"Well, it's a good thing I didn't ask for your approval then, isn't it?" Aunt Gina says. "Now, Sami, every month for quite a long time, you will bleed. That's what I mean by 'Aunt Flo' coming to visit. She visits every month for a week. I'll admit, she's quite a bad houseguest. She messes up your clothing, she makes you feel all kinds of emotions, she makes your insides feel...well, like crap. But when you're ready for children, you'll be glad she's there." She feigns a pained expression. "Well, you might still hate her."

Sami is crying again. "Every month? How am I supposed to hide this every month?" Her face is red.

"Hey, it's okay. You have me. Always come to me when you need help." She hands Sami the box. "I'm here for you."

After Sami and Aunt Gina reemerge from the bathroom, they hug. Tightly.

"Thanks, Aunt Gina," Sami whispers.

Aunt Gina kisses the top of her head. "Of course, honey."

"All good?" I ask Sami.

"All good." She takes my hand and squeezes it.

We're about to leave when Kyle bursts into the room. "Everyone is called to the chapel for a proposal announcement."

Sami tenses, her breath catching.

"Who is it?" Aunt Elizabeth looks excited, like maybe this is her chance.

Kyle hesitates, then points at us. Me, Sami and Aunt Gina.

Now

After bolting from Dr. Yen's office, I race down one hallway, then another, trying my best not to put too much weight on my bad foot. I can hear what sound like voices behind me, voices around a corner up ahead. Did someone say my name? I take a right down the nearest corridor. Ahead, there's a big steel door, a neon sign above it that says *Exit* in big red letters. I lean into the escape bar with all my body weight. Thankfully, it opens. But I'm immediately hit with a torrent of rain. It's still pouring outside. A sudden crack of thunder scares the crap out of me.

Now what, genius? I'm on the fire stairs. In a deluge. I can only go up or down. I know they'll be waiting for me at the bottom. So up it is. Gotta get to the roof. But then what? Walk across the roofs of New Jersey until I am completely out of the grasp of men with notepads and pink-haired girls who watch long, colorful movies and tired men who offer me frosted cookies? All I know is somehow I need to get myself to an airport, sneak or lie my way onto a plane, fly to California and find the others, my real family. After that, I'll run off and start a new life with them. Away from disbeliever doctors who pry and poke until they know our deepest secrets.

Sounds like a great plan.

I ignore the sarcastic voice, starting up the stairs as a flash of lightning illuminates the neighboring buildings for an instant.

The rain has already soaked through my clothes, the old sweatshirt the Tired Man gave me last week and the leggings Lauren left on the bed for me to find. My beat-up Converse sneakers, which once belonged to Aunt Jane (and are practically the only thing I have left from the compound), squish like sponges with every step I take.

I almost slip and fall a couple of times, can feel myself panicking. Who knew that fire stairs get slippery when wet?

It doesn't matter. I keep going until there are no more steps to climb. I'm on the roof. Finally.

What now?

Steam comes out of my mouth as I struggle to catch my breath.

The only other roof I can feasibly climb onto from where I am is across a six-foot chasm. I'm pretty sure I won't be able to make it.

God, I'm so stupid. This was never going to work. Even if I climbed down now and tried the roads, would I get away? No. They'd stop me. They'll always stop me. I'm never getting out of here. I'll never see my family again.

You'd be better off throwing yourself off the roof.

I stare off the edge, into the rain, into the street.

Would it feel good, in some twisted way, to jump? To just throw myself forward and let gravity pull me down? I bet all the air would leave my lungs, and my bones would snap in midair. My thoughts would disappear. It's what Augur would want me to do, lacking other options.

Easy way out.

Just a few more steps, up and forward...

"Gracelyn?"

The Tired Man's voice. I turn around, face him.

I could take a step up and jump right now. I could. He's too far away to stop me.

And yet.

The expression on his face is so full of fear.

He looks too much like Summer, and I couldn't do this to her.

He charges forward and wraps me in his soaking arms. I let him. I don't resist.

"Gracelyn, I don't even know what to say to you." He sounds almost on the verge of tears. "I know you've been through hell. I know. But I can't let you have this kind of freedom if you're gonna keep pulling sh—stuff, like this." He closes his eyes, takes a deep breath. "I'm sorry. I'm sorry. I just...I can't let you down. I can't let your parents down. Again." He puts a hand on my head. "Say something, Gracelyn. Please."

I hesitate. "I want to be with them. My family." Seeing the look of horror on his face, I add, "The ones who are still here, alive."

He lets out a loud sigh. "Gracelyn, I don't know how to tell you this, but… I am your family." The rain has slacked off, but we're both soaked to the bone.

"I know," I say, shivering.

"Do you?" He looks exhausted, wrung out.

"Yeah, you're my un—" using that word to describe him makes me want to throw up. "You're my mother's brother. You were there when I was born. And she was in that picture of you."

"I thought you forgot when I told you that."

I shake my head.

"Okay, so you know. Then why all of this? We're just trying to help."

I love my sister. My real aunts and uncles. Augur. What I feel for the Tired Man and Lauren isn't love. I don't know what it is. I just know what it isn't. So I say it. "I don't love you." And then I see the look on his face and think maybe I shouldn't have been so blunt.

He sighs. "Okay. Okay." He looks up at the sky and pinches the bridge of his nose. "Let's go home."

He leads me down the stairs to the sidewalk below, where a few police officers are waiting, their caps beaded with rain.

The Tired man talks to them for a moment, and they disperse. One of them shoots me an inquisitive look as he leaves.

We walk silently back to the car. Nathan opens his door and looks at me standing on the other side. "Get in," he says.

For some reason, I do. We drive in silence.

Home.

Back at the house, he blocks me from going upstairs. "I'm implementing a new rule. You have to spend at least two hours every day outside of your room. And you have to eat at least one meal with us. You can complain all you want, but that's what's happening."

I open my mouth, start to protest, then stop. *Just a game. It's just a game they're playing with you. That's all it ever is.* Maybe they do love me, but I can't let that change anything.

I just can't.

Three Months Before

The first wedding I remember going to was Aunt Salma's and Augur's, where Aunt Salma wore the same long beautiful white dress as Summer. After the ceremony we ate pasta with pesto sauce, garlic bread and fresh lemonade. We danced past curfew, and though we all felt tired the next morning, it was the good kind of tired.

Now, the weddings are way less fun. I guess the novelty of them has worn off over the years. Tonight, I'm wearing a ripped, old dress. We still don't know what we're eating. And curfew takes precedence over having a good time.

"You ready?" asks Fawn. I'm fussing because she has a much nicer dress than me. "If we're late, we'll be in trouble."

"You go ahead," I say. "I'll be out in a minute."

She looks anxiously at the door. "No, it's okay. I'll wait."

After a minute of frantic review, I give up. I can manage. In the hallway outside our room, lurks Uncle Hiram, who looks at us in a way I find unsettling.

"What's he doing?" I hiss.

Fawn shrugs, but I feel like she knows something she's not saying.

The dining room is packed. A few people give us "you're late" looks as we make our entrance, but since the bride and groom are nowhere in sight, we're not *technically* late. I take a seat next to Sami, who seems to be attempting to carve her initials into the table with her thumbnail.

"Hey."

"Heya," she says, without looking up.

"How long you been waiting?"

"A while. Where have you been?" She's made an S by connecting two crescent fingernail indents. She moves on to the G.

"Practicing. Augur asked me to play in his place during his dances." I say this like it's not the biggest deal ever, like I haven't been wanting to do this for years. My stomach is churning. At the same time, I'm so excited I feel like jumping up and down.

The front doors fly open suddenly, and there are Augur and Aunt Gina, holding hands, smiling. Aunt Gina's hair is piled high on top of her head, held in place with the same flower clip she wears every day.

They walk into the sea of dining tables and Augur launches into his usual speech about love, and how Gina will give him holy children, which is received with applause and cheers.

The dinner that follows is less grand. It used to be stuff like vegetable dumplings and white rice, or burgers made of kale smothered in cheese. But tonight, it's tomato soup and potatoes cut into wedges, all of it salted within an inch of its life. Even so, it's better than anything we've had in the last three weeks. Except, I'm still hungry when I finish, and no one gets seconds.

During the post-dinner cleanup, Augur nods at me from across the room to let me know I'll be playing first. My stomach does a flip. I can feel sweat blossoming under my arms.

I rush back to the children's quarters, the boards squeaking under my bare feet, and retrieve the guitar and sheet music from under my bed.

"What are you doing?" Sami's voice causes me to rear back, nearly cracking my skull on the bed frame.

"Jeez, Sami—what's it look like I'm doing?"

"It *looks like* you're bleeding." She bends down and puts her hand on my head, then she shows me the blood on her fingers.

"Well, that makes two of us," I say, rubbing my skull. No time for a Band-Aid or anything.

"Shut up."

She looks through my music while I polish and strum, laughing when she comes to one of the songs. "This is so sappy," she says.

I ignore her and start twisting the knobs.

"Something in the way she moves," she says, reading the lyrics in a dramatic tone, "attracts me like no other lover!"

She's just jealous. She's always been jealous. Don't let her annoy you. Don't let her take this away from you.

"Something in the way she woos me," she continues, reading slowly. "Don't want to leave her now..." Her face changes. She puts down the music. "Did you pick this?"

"Well, yeah, out of a book of songs Augur gave me," I say, blushing.

"I take it back," she says. "It's nice."

There's a knock at the door. Summer inches it open. "Grace, Augur says you should come now. Hey Samira."

"I'll be right there." I snatch the music out of Sami's hands and walk towards the door, not waiting to see if she follows.

When I step up onto the tables that have been pushed together to make a stage, everyone goes quiet. In fact, it's the only way they can all hear me, since the microphones don't have stands and I have to go without one.

"Hi, um...I'm going to play a song now." A few people laugh but Augur nods up at me. *You got this. Don't worry.* I take a deep breath and play the first few notes.

Augur and Aunt Gina dance together as I start to sing. My voice shakes, and my eyes wander to Uncle Oliver, who doesn't look mad, just a little nervous.

When I reach the first chorus, I see Sami enter the circle of people. She stares at me as I sing.

"Something in her style that shows me
I don't want to leave her now."

I go into the bridge, which is faster. A few other people start to slow dance, joining Augur and Aunt Gina.

Almost everyone has found someone to dance with. But Sami stands in the middle of the floor, watching me. I try not to look back, try to focus on the music.

"I don't want to leave her now
You know I believe and how."

After I finish, everyone claps politely. Augur climbs up on the table, lifts my arm. The clapping gets louder. "That was excellent, Gracelyn. Now go enjoy the celebration!"

I hop down off the table, and the rest of the band climbs up to take my place. They start playing another love song, this one even slower.

I'm just nestling my guitar safely in a corner when Sami runs into my arms, nearly knocking me over. "That was amazing!"

I feel my cheeks getting hot.

"I didn't know you were that good!"

"Oh my God, I was so nervous. Was it obvious?"

She shakes her head, no, grinning, looking out at the dance floor. "Would her ladyship like to dance?" She kneels and kisses my hand.

I blush furiously and lift her up. "It would be my honor, Princess Samira."

She drapes her arms over my shoulders. I put mine on her waist.

"That song is so pretty, who wrote it?" She asks as we sway back and forth.

"I don't know." I twirl her and she laughs. "Someone out there." I motion to the front door with my head. "I guess there are some talented disbelievers."

"Well, I'm glad they wrote it."

The music fades away, everyone else on the dance floor has become a ghost. It feels like it's just me and her, in our own pocket of the universe.

Our swaying comes to a halt. Her curls are messily pulled back into a braid that Aunt Salma did earlier. The bridge of her nose is still flaky and red from the sun. Her lips are dry and cracked. She has a scar on her jaw, from when we were eleven and she tripped on the chapel stairs. I have this weird urge to trace it with my hand. She's a few inches shorter than me, and when she looks at me, she has to look up. The moment she does that, I realize that I love her.

I think I've loved her ever since she put her orange-juice sticky hand in mine when we were six years old and declared us best friends. Or maybe I've loved her since my twelfth birthday, when she gave me a sunrise for a present. Or maybe I've just always loved her for no reason at all. All I know is that in this perfect, quiet moment, I feel that love like an explosion.

Sami's eyes go wide, and her head snaps back like I just slapped her.

"You what?"

I want to repeat it, what I must have just said out loud. But there are so many people around us.

How many of these people would kill us if I did what I want to do right now?

I remember Augur talking about homosexuality, telling us about Jared, his childhood friend. He had a girlfriend in school, he was on the football team. I don't know much about football, but I know it's manly from the way Augur talks about it. But after high school, he broke up with his girlfriend. He moved to a city that Augur compared to Babylon and slept with men. Augur said that one of the men got him sick, and Jared died. He said that it was God's punishment for Jared going against nature.

I don't want to be like Jared. And I don't want to be the reason Sami ends up like him.

So instead of repeating what I said, I push her off me, shoving her into the wall.

"Gracelyn, what the hell?" Other people turn to look at us.

Instead of apologizing, I run away. Just like I always seem to do.

"Good morning, Gracelyn."

Confession. I don't think I've felt less excited about confessing in my life.

"Good morning." I cross myself. This is my first confession in five days. I can think of about thirty sins I've committed during that time, but none that I have any plans to share. "I, uh…"

Did I tell you that Sami bled? Or that your new wife is running a secret period product ring under your nose? Or that I'm everything you warned us not to be?

"Gracelyn?"

"I'm sorry, Augur." I cross my fingers behind my back for the things I'm about to omit. "I wasted food last night. I lied to an adult about how much gardening I did. I didn't get out of bed right away this morning. I'm sorry for all my sins."

"For your penance, three rounds."

I think I'll do five.

"I absolve you of your sins."

"Amen." I cross myself with my fingers still intertwined.

"Go in peace."

Fawn comes in as I'm leaving. She looks confident. Like she isn't hiding anything. Must be nice.

I go to stand by the door, where Uncle Hiram is waiting for me. We walk out the door and down the Chapel steps. We walk across the yard, passing a line of people waiting for their confessions. We walk into the main building and down the basement stairs. There is, as always, a pan of hot pokers in the corner, under shelf upon shelf of guns.

I look down at my arm. I have three old burns on the left, and one on the right, so right arm it is.

I pick up the poker, the end only slightly hot. I clench my eyes shut and hold out my right arm.

Now

I spend a lot of my out-of-the-room time at the kitchen table, looking at magazines.

Before Augur banned everything, we only had newspapers. Magazines are infinitely more interesting. The one I like most has a woman on the front. Her skin is dark, and she has a large, glistening afro and glittery red lipstick. An invisible wind billows her long burgundy silk dress. She might be the most beautiful woman I've ever seen. The word *Vogue* is written in large letters above her head.

Opening the magazine, I'm faced with another giant picture, this one of two men, face to face, mouths slightly open, eyes closed. I quickly flip the magazine shut.

My plan was to protest the new rules by refusing to eat, but I'm weak when presented with hearty food. I haven't had much of that lately.

For tonight's dinner, the Tired Man makes pasta with meat sauce for himself and Lauren, and since I told him I don't eat meat, he puts pesto on mine. Theirs smells better, but I won't give in. I bet that the apple Eve once ate smelled amazing too.

There's an awkward stop-and-start stiffness to our dinner conversation. When Lauren complains about her English class, the Tired Man tells her she might like it better if they were reading books she enjoyed. Lauren lets his words hang in the air, and another silence ensues. It's painful.

"So, Gracelyn..." the Tired Man says, turning his attention to me.

I shoot him a look.

"Never mind," he says, backing off. Another awkward silence.

"Dad, can Violet come over tomorrow? We're practicing for the show." I appreciate Lauren's attempt to make this dinner feel less awkward, but unfortunately thus far it isn't working.

After ten more painful minutes, I excuse myself and go back to the bedroom. Closing the door, I sit down on the bed and start to pray.

God, why have you done this to me and my family? Augur said that we would be rewarded for living the way he told us to, so who was lying? You or him? Did you tell him to make us live that way just for fun? Or did he make us suffer for nothing?

This can't have all been for nothing.

Later, I go back downstairs and find Lauren doing homework at the kitchen table while listening to music on her earbuds; the Tired Man's doing his work on the living room couch with the television on but muted.

I sit quietly, observing them both.

When the news comes on, the Tired Man puts down his work and turns up the volume. The trials have been on every day and though I don't really want to watch, I also can't look away.

Aunt Elizabeth, Uncle Jim, Uncle Hiram, and Uncle Liam are all on trial. Most of them for the same four things: possession and use of illegal firearms; child abuse and neglect; conspiracy to kill federal officers; and first-degree murder.

Trials unwind slowly. According to the Tired Man, Aunt Elizabeth's has been going on for a month. I started watching Monday, now it's Friday, and I can't think about anything else. It's not that I don't believe that they did the things they did. I saw some of it happen. I just have a hard time understanding why they should be punished. Hearing the actions described makes them sound unforgivable, but I know that's not true.

Augur would forgive them. He would thank them.

Aunt Elizabeth is hard to watch, though. She's making an absolute fool of herself, blubbering continually. It's kind of pathetic. And she's facing a greater number of charges than anyone.

Uncle Jim is good at seeming honest. He admits he owned an illegally converted gun, whatever that is, and he says he had no excuse to use it on the officials who showed up that day. He just wants a do-over. He wants to give his children a new life. I almost cry when he says that. So does the Tired

Man. Uncle Hiram, on top of the other things he's charged with, has been accused of sexual abuse. I don't know what sexual abuse is, really, but I can infer, because when Lauren hears about it, she gets spitting mad.

Aunt Glinda is so old, they don't even have a trial for her. She's apparently legally blind, so she couldn't have shot anyone, and everyone else testified that she could barely walk. The judge decided she wouldn't get any time in jail but kept her there to serve as a witness, though since she's blind, I don't see how she'll be of much use.

Apparently, people want me and the other kids to testify. Which is why there were reporters and news trucks camping out when I first got here. They can't convict anyone of child abuse unless a child testifies, since none of the adults will explain themselves.

Before leaving for my Saturday session with Dr. Yen, I head down to the kitchen to make myself lunch. The Tired Man insists I get my own lunch now, since the house rule is that everyone fend for themselves. I like it. I like getting to choose what I eat. I can also go downstairs much more quickly now. Usually, the Tired Man is at the table playing solitaire with an old deck of cards or reading the paper, but today he's standing at the open front door, talking to someone. The someone sounds very urgent.

I lean over the counter to see what's going on.

A woman in a pinstripe pantsuit, with a brown bob and a pair of glasses perched atop her head, is talking animatedly, nervously rubbing together the fingers of one hand.

She notices me over the Tired Man's shoulder and stops twitching long enough to wave. Not knowing what else to do, I wave back.

The Tired Man looks at me over his shoulder, and I slide back down from the counter. He sighs audibly and beckons the woman to come inside.

They take seats at the kitchen table, and she places her briefcase in front of her. The Tired Man waves me over, pulls me into his chest and whispers, "You don't have to do anything she says, okay?" He kisses the top of my head, a poor disguise for his secretive words, then pushes me towards a chair.

"Gracelyn?" she says, as I settle into the chair across from her. "I'm Agent Amelia Hill. Lovely to meet you, finally." Government. "Do you shake hands?" She holds hers out to me. I shake it. Her hand is clammy and cold. *Ew.*

"Let's start with a bit of an explanation, shall we?" she says, not really asking a question. "I'm an FBI investigative agent. Do you know what that is?"

I almost laugh at the question, though I nod instead. *I know more about the FBI than you can imagine. I've seen slideshows. Movies. I know what kinds of guns you use, the clips that go in them, how many shots they hold, and I can spot one of you or your vehicles from a mile away.*

"Excellent!" she says. "One less thing for me to explain." She laughs a bit, as if that were funny. "Are you okay with me asking you some questions?"

It's like I'm like a little child who needs to be guided through every sentence she utters. Again, I humor her with a nod.

"Awesome." She puts her phone on the table and starts to record me. "What's your full name?"

"Gracelyn Cathrine Joan Alverb-Green." *No point in lying about that.*

"What is your date of birth?"

She continues with the basics, along with some questions about injuries or medical issues I might or might not have. "Have you ever been vaccinated for chickenpox, hepatitis b, rotavirus, diphtheria, tetanus, influenza, poliomyelitis, measles, etcetera?" She smiles, revealing a lipstick stain on her front teeth.

"I've never heard of any of that," I tell her. I think influenza is a long way of saying the flu, which I had when I was seven and again when I was twelve. Other than that, none of the terms she mentioned has any meaning for me. I do know I've never been vaccinated for anything. Another one of Augur's rules. "Vaccinations fill your body with poisons."

Agent Hill checks to make sure that her phone is recording everything I'm saying. Satisfied, she looks up at me again.

"Gracelyn, are you aware that in three weeks, Fawn and Juniper Green will be going on national television to testify against all senior members of the Church of the Holy Saviors, excluding Glinda and Jim Green?"

What?

"I was not aware," I say, trying to hide my shock. Augur told us some people would turn, betray. But I never expected it to be Fawn.

"What I want from you is very simple," she says. "I want you to testify with them." *Of course she does.* "You can refuse, but it would be of immense help to the FBI if you cooperated. I know this might be hard to hear, but some of these people deserve to go to jail for the rest of their lives. We need your help to make that happen."

Hard to hear? What the hell is wrong with you?

"It'll be an ordeal, I won't lie to you. You'll have to fly out to California and go on national television. We can obscure your identity, but ultimately, people may find out who you are. Again, as I say, whether or not you agree to do this is up to you and your uncle. You should know, though, that whatever misgivings you might have, you'd be doing the right thing, and hopefully, it will help you in your healing process."

It's not like I don't see what her game is. Still. California. I could go to California and see everyone. *Are you actually considering this? No. Not under any circumstances!*

"Would I be testifying with Fawn and Juniper?"

Her shark grin reappears. She thinks I'm considering it. *Are you?*

"Your testimony would be in whatever format would make you feel most comfortable." *How about no format? How about with a piece of gaffer's tape over your mouth? You can't possibly be considering this.*

"So, what do you say?"

That's when the Tired Man swoops in. "We'll think about it, Agent Hill. Thanks for all your help!" He gathers her things and practically shoves her out the door, thrusting her still-recording phone into her hands. "We'll see you again soon." He slams the door closed behind her before she can object or say goodbye or anything.

"That woman is never coming into this house again." He looks at me. "You do not have to go to California."

"I know," I say.

The Tired Man lets me skip therapy, and I risk seeming less shaken up than he thinks I am by asking if I can still have my call with the other kids.

The little ones are playing with something called a switch, and are apparently so enthralled by it that they won't even talk to me. Fawn, of course, gets on first.

"You're going to testify?" I say, almost the second she speaks. I hear her fumble with the phone, probably taking it off speaker.

"Say it a little louder, would you?" she hisses.

"Well, are you?"

"Yes."

"Why would you do that? Hasn't our family suffered enough without you blabbing all our business?" I feel bad for guilting her, but not bad enough to stop.

"I wouldn't have agreed to do it, except... Uncle Hiram is on trial."

What does that have to do with anything?

"I'm sorry, Gracelyn. It has nothing to do with you or anyone else in our family." She takes a shaky breath. "I'm... I mean I *was—*"

"Fawn, just tell me." I'm becoming impatient with people who withhold information from me these days.

"I was pregnant, Gracie," she says, voice barely a whisper. "When I got here, I was pregnant with Uncle Hiram's baby."

Two Weeks Before

I can feel paranoia in the air. Sami would tell me that *I'm* the one being paranoid, but I swear I can feel something. It's got me on edge.

Augur's been extending his nightly talks and becoming increasingly harsh in dealing with perceived infractions. There are whispered complaints about the length of the sermons, but no one's got the courage to say anything to him.

Sleep deprivation is new to us. We've always been given enough time to rest so that we'll be able to focus, work hard, and have fun when allowed. But these days, it feels like there's no time for fun at all. And even when there is, I'm too tired to take advantage, or my arms are too sore from repentance. Sometimes I can't even play the guitar. Augur's explanation is that he's been coddling us up till now, letting us live in luxury. Meanwhile, as we get soft, the disbelievers grow stronger, waiting to attack. He's not going to coddle us anymore.

I guess that makes sense, but I'm tired.

We're digging in the garden today because we need more space to plant crops, and I'm getting a headache from the heat. The smell of tired sweat drifts through the air. I hear people grunting more than usual.

Summer looks worn out and frail, putting seeds in the ground. I'm worried she'll fall over.

I poke Aunt Lillian, who's digging next to me and give her a "can you please switch places with me?" look. She nods, and I make my way down the line to Summer.

"Hey, are you all right?" I whisper, nudging her so she'll look at me.

I see something in her eyes that scares me. It's exhaustion, clearly, but there's something else. Pride, love—whatever it is, I don't like it.

"I'm fine Grace, why?" She forces a smile.

"You just look kind of tired. Did you sleep at all last night?" I don't need to ask, because I know the answer. We were all up for hours. I put my hand on her arm.

"I'm fine, Gracelyn. Worry about yourself." She goes back to seeding.

"I'm sorry Summer, you just look really—"

"Grace, for God's sake, stop!" She suddenly hauls off and slaps me, knocking me backward so hard that I stumble on the uneven ground and fall on my butt. My mouth tastes coppery with blood.

Summer's hit me before. When I was eight, I was obsessed with throwing things as far as I could, and I broke one of the chapel windows with a rock. And then again, when I was eleven, she got pissed about a prank Sami and I pulled. But she's never hit me this hard before. My cheek pulses with pain, and I can feel the loose tooth in the back of my mouth has gotten even looser.

She stands over me, not looking remorseful at all. I stop myself from crying and just stare at her, like she's someone I don't even know.

Aunt Elizabeth grabs my arm roughly and helps me to my feet. "What just happened?"

I don't say anything. Summer doesn't either. Standing, I'm taller than her.

I spit bloody saliva at her feet. She doesn't flinch.

Someone says something about getting me some ice. Fawn volunteers to take me to the main building. I hear murmurs of encouragement, and Fawn spins me around and marches me towards the building.

"God, what a bitch," she says under her breath.

I laugh, forgetting for a second how much pain I'm in.

When we reach the main building, Aunt Reina, with her messy bun and white apron, gives me ice, not asking what it's for. I thought she might mention the red handprint on Fawn's arm, but she doesn't.

She sees the bags under our eyes, which hardly rival her own. She always has to be available, most hours of the day and night. Still, she says we should stay there, maybe sleep off the heat on her cots. Lying down, gratefully, we drift off, imagining another world, somewhere far from here.

Now

My mind is racing.

I've been sleeping well—almost too well—since I got here, but tonight I can't seem to turn off my brain.

I was never a good sleeper at home. I used to climb into Summer's bed during thunderstorms, and still I wouldn't be able to fall asleep for hours. God, I hated those storms. Everyone always told me I'd outgrow the fear, but I never did. When Summer moved to the wives' quarters I'd just lay in my bed for hours, waiting, praying for the storm to be over. I didn't tell anyone because I knew it made me seem like a baby. When we were about eleven, Sami woke up one night and saw me lying there, counting back from one hundred for the fifth time. She climbed into my bed and lay there with me until we both fell asleep. We didn't talk about it the next morning, but from then on, whenever there was thunder, she'd silently tiptoe across the room, and in the morning, she'd be gone. We never had to discuss it, never spoke while we were lying there together. I would just hold on to the warmth of her presence, the feeling that someone cared, and the feeling that maybe I didn't have to grow out of anything, it was okay to be afraid.

Tonight, I'm not scared, just overwhelmed. My head is so full of thoughts it feels like it might explode. One hundred and fourteen ghosts are screaming at me. I see Uncle Hiram's eyes flitting to Fawn as she sits, twelve years old and blushing in a bathroom.

Uncle Hiram.

Every time I think about him, I burn with anger.

Fawn told me everything in static whispers this afternoon, careful not to let the other kids hear her. She told me how she realized he was watching her when she was about thirteen. That at first, she'd liked the attention, but eventually, she began to get scared. She told me how he would touch her, and, if she pushed him away, he'd clamp his hands on her until it hurt. He'd lure her to the bathrooms or to his bed. She wanted to say no, but she thought he would snap her wrists or worse. When she got pregnant, she didn't even know. She'd always had a sensitive stomach, so at first, she thought it was that. It was the government doctors who told her about the baby. That was when she broke down and told them everything. She was scared, especially of them, but she knew she had to tell the truth. How she wasn't ready to have a baby and how she never wanted to think about Uncle Hiram again. That was why she killed the baby.

Augur told us you should never ever get rid of a baby. A baby is a blessing, no matter what the circumstances. But I understand why she did it. I would probably have done the same thing.

Good for you, you formed a thought of your own.

Fawn cried a lot while telling me what had happened. I'm pretty much out of tears these days, but listening to *her* cry had me on the edge of losing it. The pain in her voice.

The headlights of passing cars create square panels of light on the wall above my bed. The tires ring through puddles from the earlier rain.

I throw the blanket off, swing my legs over the edge of the bed, and plant my feet on the rug.

Sometimes, I go into the Tired Man's room just to look around or snoop. But his computer is gone. I don't know what he's done with it. I do know where there's another one, however.

In Lauren's room.

I ease the door open so as not to make any noise. I know the Tired Man and Lauren are awake downstairs, watching a show. Across the hallway, I open the door to Lauren's room, then close it slowly behind me, wincing as it squeaks.

In the dark, I feel along the wall for a light switch; the room brightens suddenly at my touch, forcing me to squint. It's a risk to turn on the lights, but I don't have any other option.

Lauren's computer is on top of her desk, against the far wall. I slide into her desk chair and lift open the top, which is decorated with psychedelic 3-D stickers. The screen lights up. It's asking for a password. Damn it.

Why can't anything be simple?

I look around the desk for clues.

Pasted to the wall above is a collage of pictures. Tiny stickers secure some, but others are stuck to the wall with Scotch tape. I see George and Violet in a couple of the photos. I also see a bunch of people I don't recognize.

I flip open one of the sketchbooks stacked on Lauren's desk and see drawings of flowers and rocks and the lake behind the house. *She's really good at this.*

Next, I check the drawers. I'm feeling a little guilty looking through her things. Not guilty enough to stop, though.

There's a translucent orange bottle in the first drawer. The label reads, "Prescription for Spicer, Lauren." I turn it around and see that it says "Lexapro. Take once daily."

I put it back in the drawer and pull out some other papers, sifting through them, looking at each one briefly.

Nothing.

I slump back into her chair and shove the heels of my hands into my eyes.

What am I even doing?

In the trashcan under the desk, there's an empty box of hair dye for a color called "electric magenta." Interesting. As I raise my eyes, I notice that there's a narrow drawer under the desktop just above my legs that I hadn't realized was there.

Opening it, I find a single piece of paper folded twice.

I open it.

A messy scrawl reads:

comp-pw: alex123.

Thank you, Lauren. Thank you for being stupid.

I click the trackpad and the computer lights up again.

I type "alex123." The screen goes dark for a second, then changes to a background of Lauren and Violet wrapped in a towel at the beach, laughing. There are a ton of little icons on the screen that don't really look like apps, so I ignore them.

We had a computer when I was really little. Augur got rid of it because he said the government had been using it to track us down, but I still remember using the explore function to search for coloring pages to print out.

The day he took away the computer, I cried. That was our last connection to the outside that wasn't a news station. I always cried when he took things away. Like when we stopped getting any stations except the news because Augur found about fifteen people all watching a show about Jewish people who lived in New York. He said it was for the best, but still I wept. And when he burned all our books, I cried again, and he told Summer that if he ever saw me cry again, he'd lock me in the basement for a week.

I never cried in front of an adult after that.

This computer looks like it's hardly even related to the one we had. Every app icon is different now, and it all looks less grainy.

I click on what looks most familiar, the icon for Safari.

The blinking cursor is back again.

I immediately type in "coloring pages" and hit the enter button, just to see if it works the same way ours did.

In a flash, a whole new page pops up, with the same kind of coloring pages I used to print out. Right away, I see one of my favorite characters to color, a mermaid with long hair.

I click on the search bar again.

Gracelyn Green

Immediately, the screen changes again. Several pictures of the Tired Man greet me. A blue headline reads: **Relative of Potential Witness in the Randolph Milly Investigation Refuses to Meet with Press.** Underneath that is another blue headline saying the same thing, but angrier. Apparently, people also search for: **Randolph Milly, Church of The Holy Saviors Tragedy, Who was Randolph Milly?** and **Hiram Green.**

I click on the first blue headline.

I jump a bit when the screen changes completely, though I'm not sure what I expected to happen.

I read the whole article, which leads me to a different article, then another and another, until I wind up on a site called Wikipedia, reading about the history of Guyana.

My head is spinning again. Every article insists that almost all the members of my family who are on trial deserve to be in jail. Some insist I should testify against them; some don't want me or the rest of the kids to have to think about any of this ever again; some are very angry at us; some are angry at Augur; the first one I read was angry at the Tired Man.

Augur would love this.

Sami would hate it.

She always loathed being the center of attention for anything, even when she'd done something spectacular. I would give her a compliment, and she'd act like I'd committed a crime. She would *never* testify. She would *never* go on tv and tell the world what happened to our family. She wouldn't want to put our family through that, and she wouldn't want to get in front of a camera. I type in her name anyway.

Samira Green

Not as much comes up for her, maybe because she has doctors shielding her from the world. There is one picture of her. It seems like it's the day of the siege, and she's sitting in an ambulance, clutching a cup of water like it's the only thing keeping her alive. Behind her, I can see the chapel in flames. There's blood in her hair, and a burn cuts across her arm. Ash is streaked on her hands and her face.

She's smiling.

She looks happier than I've ever seen her, not like you would expect a kid to look while their home burns to the ground behind them. I feel a pinprick of betrayal, but mostly I just have questions. So many questions.

I click away from the photo and go back to the search bar. Typing in my own name, not one picture of me comes up.

Next, I try:

How to get to California

Two Weeks Before

W hen Fawn and I wake up, we hear the dinner bell ringing in the chapel. After the nap, I feel refreshed. Also starving.

The moment we arrive in the dining hall, Aunt Elizabeth berates us for being late, on top of the fact we've been missing all afternoon. She doesn't haul off and slap us, probably because she witnessed what happened earlier, but she wags her finger at us as we stare at the floor and say, "Yes, Aunt Elizabeth," over and over. When she finally lets us go, we rush to get in line at the food table.

Dinner today is just rice with two browning apple slices on the side. I hate brown rice, but I gobble it down as fast as I can since I missed lunch. I savor the dry apple slices, not talking to anyone. No one is talking to anyone today.

After getting some sleep I feel sharper, but everybody else still seems slow, ponderous. They eat their food in unison, like factory workers on an assembly line. Rice grains cover the table. No one brushes them up.

Sami is sitting fifteen people down from me on the other side of the table. She keeps looking over, and I keep ignoring her. A voice in my head tells me how mean it is to pretend she's not right there, but I override it.

After I finish eating, I take my plate to the kitchen and scrape it clean, then leave it in the sink for whoever is on dish duty. I can see some of the little kids sitting in the corner, blowing bubbles with dish soap, using their hands. Aunt Glinda is keeping an eye on them from a chair over in the corner. Even if we were getting enough sleep she would still be sleeping through the day.

One of the kids, Genji, is wearing a shirt that once belonged to me. My mom got it a long time ago; it advertises a band called The Clash.

Back in the dining hall, I take my seat and pick at the edge of my thumbnail.

Something pelts against my shoulder. A balled-up napkin. I unball it and see writing inside.

Can we talk?

I look at Sami, who's giving me a pleading look. She tosses me a pen. I scribble

Where?

on the napkin, roll it up and throw it back at her, along with the pen. A few moments later the balled-up napkin comes sailing back.

Bathroom?

Five minutes later I'm sitting on the closed toilet lid when Sami comes in. She keeps her distance, leaning against the door, just looking at me.

"What?"

She just kind of shrugs.

"Since you apparently don't have anything to talk about, I guess I'm gonna leave," I say. I get up but she blocks my way.

"Gracie," she says, "Can we please talk?"

I try to push my way past her, but she doesn't move. "Fine, you're the one who called this meeting, so talk."

Nothing.

"That's what I thought." I try to leave again.

"Gracie, please, help me out here. What happened at the wedding?"

"Nothing. Seriously, Sami, get a grip."

Sami sighs, exasperated. "Look. Can we please just forget it? I don't care about all that...stuff. I don't want to be mad at you."

Stuff. How can she not care?

"Okay. We can forget it."

Sami nods, and we leave the bathroom together.

At chapel, we get a heavy dose of the Book of Revelations. When I was little, I couldn't handle the descriptions of lakes of blood and fire, and I would pray the whole time, begging God that I wouldn't have to see it one day. Over the years, I stopped worrying as much, but today, I'm feeling extra sinful, and I pray just as hard as I used to.

God, I know that today I disrespected my sister, and I've done so many other sinful things. I'm so sorry. I know the end times are coming soon, and all I want is to die when they do. That's all I've ever wanted. Please forgive me, God, just let me go to heaven. I know I've sinned. And I know that I don't deserve it. But please.

Please.

Even when the clock hits midnight, Augur isn't tired. He seems crazed, his knuckles bleeding from pounding the lectern. Spit flies from the corners of his mouth.

"But the cowardly, the unbelieving, the vile, the murderers, the sexually immoral, those who practice magic arts, the idolaters and all liars–they will be consigned to the fiery lake of burning sulfur. That is the second death."

Summer looks at him, rapt, eyes wide with love, devotion and fear. I wonder if mine look the same.

"And the *devil*, who deceived them, was thrown into the lake of burning sulfur, where the beast and the false prophet had been thrown. They will be tormented day and night for ever and ever."

The false prophet. I wonder about that a lot. How do you know if someone is a false prophet? The man in front of me is a real one, everyone says that, but how can we be sure? The only way to be certain would be to ask God, but you'd have to be a prophet yourself to actually hear his answer.

"It's an enigma."

The whole chapel goes quiet. Did I say that out loud?

"Gracelyn? Did you say something?" Augur asks, looking right at me. I desperately shake my head, but Summer gives me away.

"She said, 'enigma,' Augur." She looks so excited to speak with him you'd never know that they're married with a daughter. It's as if he's a celebrity on the outside that she's never spoken to.

Augur quotes a totally different part of the bible without even looking at it: "Because that excellent spirit, knowledge and understanding, interpretation of dreams, and showing of *enigmas*, and loosing of knots was found in him, in Daniel, whose name the king made Belteshazzar: now let Daniel be called, and the interpretation he doth show."

I should have kept my mouth shut.

"Perhaps rather than the punishments inflicted on the human race, maybe you'd like to hear more about the prophets. I happen to know a lot about that."

A few people laugh. "But I think that Gracelyn might need to hear more about the punishments that could await *us*. Or maybe about the sins we commit."

He's still looking at me with those almost yellow eyes, flipping through the bible in front of him. He starts reading again.

"Then one of the seven angels who had the seven bowls came and said to me, 'Come, I will show you the judgment of the great prostitute who is seated on many waters, with whom the kings of the earth have committed sexual immorality, and with the wine of whose sexual immorality the dwellers on earth have become drunk.' And he carried me away in the Spirit into a wilderness, and I saw a woman sitting on a scarlet beast that was full of blasphemous names, and it had seven heads and ten horns. The woman was arrayed in purple and scarlet, and adorned with gold and jewels and pearls, holding in her hand a golden cup full of abominations and the impurities of her sexual immorality. And on her forehead was written a name of mystery: 'Babylon the great, mother of prostitutes and of earth's abominations.'"

My face is red. I know what he's trying to tell me. If I don't shut up, there's a room in hell with my name on it.

Now

Lauren comes into my room, computer cradled in her arms.

Oh, you've really done it now, haven't you? She sits down on the edge of the bed, opens it and types in her password.

She clicks the touchpad a few times, and then turns the computer to face me. "Did you do this?" A list of my searches from the other night is on the screen.

"How did you—"

"Dude, there's this thing called a search history," she says, cutting me off. "So, we have to talk about this."

"No, we don't." My tone is sharp and a bit meaner than I intended.

Lauren seems unfazed. "If you're planning on running away," she says, "we need to talk about it."

I blow a strand of hair away from my mouth. "Look, you don't have to worry. I have no idea how to get to California, so I'm not going." I'm not lying. My search about getting to California wasn't much help. I couldn't find any directions that made sense to me.

Lauren looks at the searches, then back at me.

"I'm not here to stop you," she says. "Don't worry about that. I want to help you get there."

Excuse me, what?

"My spring break starts next week. There's a bus that takes about three days from here to L.A. I don't really know how to get to where your friends are from the bus, but we can figure that out later. I'm sure Dad will try to find us, but hopefully, if I delete the tracking app on my phone, he won't be able to."

"You really think that could work? I mean, he's not stupid," I say.

"You're right, he's not. And frankly, I have no idea. I'm also not sure if I have enough money for the bus—or a motel when we get there. I also don't know if they'll let you visit anyone since we really can't call ahead to confirm because they might tell Dad. Not only that, but I'm supposed to be with my mom that week, so she's a factor, too. I doubt Dad would send the police after us because..." she motions at me, "well you know. I don't think he want you around law enforcement who have guns." She coughs. "But yeah, basically this is kind of an insane thing to do."

It really is. "Lauren, if you... I mean, you don't have to do this if you don't want to." I'm surprised at the sincerity in my own voice.

Lauren bursts into laughter, which shocks me. "Are you kidding?" she says, "I've never wanted to do anything more in my life! Who doesn't want to go on an adventure?"

For the first time in a long time, I let loose a genuine laugh, too.

Lauren looks shocked.

"Okay," I say, "so tell me the whole plan."

The next day, Violet and George come over, and the three of them crowd into my room. Violet and George are going to stay back here and do damage control, as much as they can. I don't know why they want to help me, but they're all bursting with energy and I'm not about to discourage them.

The Tired Man interrupts our meeting to take me to therapy, commenting on the drive over that "it's nice that you're making friends." I'd like to respond that my only "friends" are his daughter and her compatriots, and there's no way I'd be friends with these people if he hadn't locked me in a house with them, but considering that he has just created an excuse for hanging out with Lauren and her friends, I keep my mouth shut.

"I think it's time for us to talk about your parents."

Dr. Yen is growing a mustache. I think I hate it.

"I already told you, they died a long time ago. Not much to talk about."

"Well, how did they die?"

"Oh, attacked by bears, I think."

He stops to write something down. "Gracelyn, I know this is difficult, but making light of it won't help."

He's right. That was mean. "My mom died giving birth to me. Well, you know, like... after. Infection or something. I don't know what it was."

"And your dad?"

"I think he had cancer. But he wasn't allowed to go get help."

"Did that happen a lot?"

"Well, there was Abel. But that was different."

"Abel..." He looks up at me from his paper.

"Aunt Jane's son. He got injured and then he died. I mean, they tried to help him, but we couldn't take him outside. But it's a little different. Abel died from his infection."

"Your dad's cancer didn't kill him?" It's weird to hear him say it.

"No. I guess he didn't really want to suffer, so I think he shot himself." I look at a tiny stain on the couch arm. "But Augur told us he left us to live a life of sin because he didn't love us."

"Us being you and Summer?"

"Mmhm. And everyone else."

"Why do you think Augur said that?"

I bristle. "I don't know. I don't presume to know why he did anything."

"You don't seem sure about that."

You're not *sure.* "I don't know. I guess when I found out the truth, I was mad? I mean, I spent a lot of time thinking my dad didn't love me. And I guess it's like, he didn't want to die slowly, and I feel like that's one of *my* biggest fears. A long, painful death." I pause. "But I guess Augur did it because he didn't want us to leave. I guess it would look bad on him if he told us he died because he wasn't allowed to get help."

"Does it look bad on him?"

"What?"

"Does it make you think less of him that he didn't let your father get the medical help he needed?"

I hold back a laugh. "There's a lot of stuff that made me think less of him, way more than that."

"Like what?"

"Like marrying Summer."

I can see his eyes sparkle at the mention of her name. "Why did that make you think less of him?"

Isn't it obvious? "I mean, she was fifteen. And she was my sister. I missed her. I have no idea if he made her happy. I mean, he made her happy in a...religious sense. Who doesn't want to be married to God?"

"You didn't."

I look down at my shoes. "No. I didn't."

"Why not?"

"Because he was old." Dr. Yen laughs. "And I didn't want...I didn't want to sleep with him. Or have children. Yet." I blush.

"Well, you're very young Gracelyn. I understand."

"Sure. But it also felt inevitable. It was a rule, you know?"

"Like not being able to leave the compound for medical help."

Yes, that is an example of a rule. Good deduction, Dr. Yen.

"It seems like the rules affected you pretty badly. None of them were very positive for you." He adjusts his glasses. "Why did you keep following them? Why didn't you leave?"

"You say that like it's simple."

"Isn't it?"

"No." I'm angry suddenly. I wish I could stop my emotions from doing this, from getting the better of me so easily. "I mean, my sister was there. And where would I even go? Seriously. I was fourteen, and I was all alone. I'd never heard of Nathan or Lauren. I was living in the middle of the fucking desert." *I just swore in front of an adult.* "I'd never interacted with a human being that didn't live on the compound. And then there was Sami—"

Dr. Yen raises his eyebrows.

Breathe. "I just don't know what I would have done."

"Correct me if I'm wrong, but that sounds deliberate. As if everything was designed to make you stay."

"Maybe. I guess. Like, I kind of thought, what if he's right? We were too scared to leave because of what might happen to us if we made it out, and what might happen if we came back."

There's silence, and then his alarm goes off. Dr. Yen looks up from his notes and smiles. I recoil. "What are you making that face for?"

"We've just made a lot of progress, Gracelyn, and I'm proud of you."

Oh god. I don't want him to be proud of me. Or... do I? Do I like Dr. Yen? *God forbid.*

"Okay, well, I'm going to leave now."

I shuffle toward the door, but before I leave, I hear him say, "You're healing, Gracelyn. It's painful. But you're not alone."

Two Weeks Before

I know things are getting tense, because this is more target practice than we've ever had. Three hours of practice four times a week, that's the new rule. I'm so exhausted I can hardly hold up my arms, but I hit the target a few times, imagining that it's Summer's head.

I'm shocked by my own thoughts. I don't want to hurt Summer. I don't.

The wind picks up and dust clouds the air. Eve and Dawn are asleep on the bench, with Abraham nestled between them. Whatever bits of hair have escaped from Sami's ponytail are glued to her face with sweat. The heat and dust are intense, even for here. How can it be this hot at the end of December?

Maybe it's the lakes of fire rising. Augur has been preaching about the end times so much lately, it feels like they could happen tomorrow.

Sami's cheek is smudged with dirt. I keep looking over at her, searching her eyes for a clue. *Is she still mad at me?*

I know I shouldn't think too much about what happened. I know I shouldn't have said what I said. She told me everything was fine, but I can't stop thinking, and I can't undo what I've done.

Augur steps onto the shooting grounds and every gun stops. No one wants him to get hurt accidentally, although I guess having *children* around active guns isn't a problem.

"Brothers and sisters, I appreciate you all complying with the new practice schedule. I know you all want to protect me and your fellow family members."

"Yes, Augur," we all mumble. I can't deny that I'm annoyed by the fact that he stands there untouched, while we're covered in sweat and dust and black grease.

That's just how it works around here.

He smiles at us lovingly, but there's a twinge of mania in his voice when he speaks. "The time is quickly approaching when we'll ascend to a higher plane. We'll soon be with God. But to get there we will have to battle the disbelievers that crawl the earth beyond our gates. Not with our minds, but with our strength. And guns, of course." Uneasy laughter. We all know he's not kidding. "I urge each of you to follow the steps we've laid out. None of you want to be left behind, do you?"

"No, Augur," we all say, shaking our heads.

He smiles. Then he leaves.

I need water. I excuse myself, letting Aunt Deirdre take my spot and run towards the main building, my feet stirring up a cloud of dust with every step.

In the kitchen, I latch on to the tap with my mouth and gulp down water so fast it trickles over my face and neck. To me, the water here has always tasted off, like there's something in it that shouldn't be there. But it's not like there are other choices. When I turn around, wiping my mouth with my wrist, Augur is right there in my face. His loving smile is gone.

"Augur, uh, it was so inspiring to listen to you—I mean, um, it's always inspiring but—" he cuts me off, grabbing my ear. "Ow!" I shriek. He claps his other hand over my mouth.

"Listen here, you little whore. I know what happened the other day."

My heart's pounding now.

"And if you do anything like that again, so help me, I will make sure you spend the rest of your life locked in the basement. Understand?"

I nod, my entire body shaking.

"You need to respect my wife. You made her look like a fool."

Wait. What?

"Just keep your mouth shut." He lets go of my ear and I recoil, banging my lower back against the sink.

I'll take that. If he doesn't know my actual secrets, maybe God will never find out. Maybe I can still be saved.

He walks away, his clean shiny boots thumping against the floor.

I reach up to touch my ear. It stings to be touched. When I look at my fingers, there's blood on them.

Sami's head pops into the kitchen. "Hey, what's going on in here?"

It takes me a moment to hear her question. My heart is still pounding out of my chest. I put a hand over my ear, hoping she won't see the blood. "Nothing."

"Are you sure?"

"Yes, Sami. God. I have to go back."

"Gracelyn—" It's strange to hear her say my full name.

"Just leave me alone!" I run past her, back toward the shooting range.

It's not Summer anymore—now I'm imagining someone else's face on the target.

Now

Though he doesn't know it, this is the last session I'll be having with Dr. Yen before I go to California. I think he can tell that I'm nervous. After our last time, I didn't really want to go back, but I thought it would be suspicious if I didn't. And anyway, I have other things to worry about.

The past week has been full of planning and talking—more talking than I've done in a long time—and lying. So much lying.

"I have a really important prompt for you today, Gracelyn."

"Oh?" I'm so preoccupied, I barely take in his words. He's got a new pink flower in the glass vase, replacing the dying orchid that was here last time.

"I want to know about the things that make you happy."

I scrunch up my face.

"Or things that have made you happy in the past."

"Why does it matter?"

"I want to hear about your life, your interests, the things you enjoy," he says, adjusting his glasses. "It doesn't have to be all doom and gloom. If you want, we could *exchange* interests. Like we're just friends talking."

I might as well indulge him, it's my last session for a while. "I like to play the guitar." I correct myself. "I liked to play the guitar."

"My brother plays the guitar!" he exclaims, desperately trying to connect with me. "When did you start playing?"

"When I was twelve. Augur showed me the basics, but then I taught myself."

"How long has it been since you played?"

"A while. The last time was Aunt Gina's wedding," I lie.

"Aunt Gina? Are you talking about Gina Locet?"

How does he know? "Yeah, I guess."

"What did you play?"

"I don't remember." *Another lie.*

"Okay." He scribbles something in his notebook. "My turn. I like to fish. But we don't cook them. Normally, I just throw them back." He takes a picture from a drawer and hands it to me. In it, he's standing in the back of a boat, holding a large fish. He's smiling. Does everyone out here have a photo like this? I hand it back to him.

"Is there anything else?"

"I don't think so. We worked all day, you know. We had Bible study, shooting practice, wrestling...lessons. On our free days I just hung out with—I just hung out. I watched the news sometimes. But there wasn't much time for fun."

"Did you ever want more than that?"

"No. I mean, maybe, but that was all I knew. Okay?" Suddenly, tears fill my eyes. "I've never gone on a boat and caught a fish. I've watched movies. I've never made friends at school. Maybe that makes my life horrible. But it wasn't all horrible. I had my sister, my family. I had my friends." I look at him, his hand and pen hovering over the pad of paper. "And now I have nothing." I cross my arms and slump down on the couch.

"Gracelyn, I am so sorry."

I'm taken aback. I didn't expect him to apologize.

"You deserve all of those things," he says. "If you want them. But you were born into a life that never gave you the opportunity for anything else. And for that I am sorry. Truly sorry."

"I-I." I'm flustered. "Thank you. I guess."

"You can still do all of those things if you want to. There will be a school for you, there will be boats for you to go on. You have time, Gracelyn. Not every moment has to count. The world isn't ending anytime soon."

I burst into tears. Instead of looking horrified, Dr. Yen offers me the box of tissues. I take one, telling him I'm sorry.

"You have nothing to apologize for. I'll say it again, Gracelyn. You have time. All the time you need, all the time you want. No one can take that away from you. You deserve time to heal, time to love, time to learn. Everyone deserves time."

Fresh tears waterfall down my face, but I wipe them away. "Thank you." I blow my nose. When I've wiped my face and taken some deep breaths, I remember something else that used to make me happy. "You know, I also like to dance."

"I like to dance too. My wife signed us up for salsa lessons last year, and at first, I was skeptical, but now I love them. We'll have to take a break from the lessons for a while because of the baby. I'll be sad about that, but..." He shrugs and smiles. "What kind of dancing did you do?"

"Just for fun. Nothing with a name. At weddings with Sami, mostly."

"Have you talked to her recently?"

"Sami?" I tense up. "No."

"Why not?"

I shrug, crossing my arms across my chest.

"Gracelyn, I've been holding back on saying this, but I think you can handle it. It seems odd to me that you won't talk about your relationship with Sami. It's clear that you two were very close. Will you at least tell me why you won't talk about her?"

He wants to know? *I won't talk about her because, even though we weren't speaking when that day happened, I was still worried about her. And I was terrified that she had died, horrified by the idea that she'd died hating me. Even though she's alive, I still panic about her all the time. I can't talk about her. If I do, I think I might just fall apart.*

"Gracelyn—"

"My time is up." I grab my jacket and leave.

I walk towards the Tired Man in the waiting room. "Gracelyn, what's going on? Are you okay?"

"What do you think?" I mumble.

The Tired Man, puzzled, looks back at the door to Dr. Yen's office, but then he says, "Okay, let's get you home," and leads me out of the building.

When we get back to the house, I stay outside, not wanting to go in. I'm certain that the Tired Man is watching me through the window as I perch on the porch swing, but I don't care. The swing reminds me of the one us kids kept begging Augur to buy us when we were little—though he never did.

Lauren comes outside after a while. Her hair is the same color as the model on the box that was in her wastebasket.

I shiver as she sits down beside me on the swing.

"Why don't you trust me?" she asks.

"What?"

She turns to look at me. "I'm doing all this stuff for you, and you don't trust me at all." She lowers her voice to a whisper. "I'm taking you to California. I'm spending my own money. I'm betraying my dad's trust for you, but you still treat me like a stranger."

"I—"

"You think this is easy for me?" she says. "You think I know exactly what to do when some cousin I've never met shows up? I mean, I always wanted a sister and I know we're not really sisters, but I want to help and understand; I've tried so hard, and you give me nothing." Her hands are shaking with anger.

She's right. I know that. I don't know where this is coming from, but she's right. Maybe the anxiety of the trip is getting to her.

"I know you barely care, so let me tell you what's going on," she continues. "Now all my dad will talk about—all he thinks about—is you. He started smoking again, and he and my mom fight on the phone so often it's like they never got divorced."

"At least you have parents," I whisper.

"What?"

"At least you have parents! I have nothing. And no one."

She's shocked into silence, and I immediately feel bad. I soften my voice. "It's not like I don't appreciate everything you've been doing for me, but I can't be some particular way just because you want me to. I need time, and I'm sorry if I hurt your feelings, but there's a lot going on with me."

Lauren ducks her head and whispers that she's sorry.

"It's...it's okay. I'm sorry, too. I shouldn't have shouted."

"No, no, I deserved that."

I turn fully toward her, and she immediately wraps her arms around me, squeezing me tight.

"I was just...being selfish, I guess."

For some reason, her saying that makes me feel guilty. "No, I... I've also been selfish. You're allowed." The hug is weird, but I probably owe her one.

"Yeah," Lauren says, pulling away. "But I'm not allowed to be a jerk. And just so you know. You don't have nothing. You have me. You have my dad. Whether you like it or not."

Two Weeks Before

"Tf the enemy captures you, do everything you can to get away. Unless we tell you otherwise, and we won't."

Uncle Dan is giving us a lesson we've had drilled into us countless times before. But today I detect a strange edge in his voice. I feel on edge, too. I can't tell if it's just because everyone's exhausted from all the work we've been doing, or if, for me, it's from my recent loss of sleep.

"If you have no way to escape, then killing yourself becomes the only option. You can't allow them to keep you and control you. It's better to be dead than to give yourself over. The disbelievers will do anything to keep you alive, because they want what you have. They want to be holy and pure."

"Life is a blessing, as I always tell you," adds Augur, who's looking on. "But it isn't a blessing in this scenario, it's the last thing you want."

"The best way is to shoot yourself or cut open your carotid artery. A slash across the throat, quick and easy." Uncle Dan makes a slashing motion with his hand. "But more painful than blowing your brains out, eh, Augur?"

Augur chuckles and nods.

"And you can also kill *them*. Stabbing is best, but you can also strangle them. Depending on the size of the person, that could be better." Uncle Dan says this like he's describing the best way to cook a potato.

Mary is crying, like she always does at these meetings. She's nearly melting into a puddle of tears at my side, getting my shirt all wet and snotty. I wrap my arm around her anyway and pull her close.

Augur notices me practically smothering Mary to hide her tears. He comes over, kneeling in front of us. "Let her go, Gracelyn," he says.

"But—"

"Let her go."

When Mary looks at Augur, she starts crying harder. He softens his face so that he's the kind man we all know, and cups her head in his hands, wiping the tears off her cheeks with his thumbs.

"Mary, you know I can't shield you from the truth."

She nods shakily.

"You can't hide in Gracelyn's shirt when she's drowning in the lakes of fire. What if she dies? Then who will protect you? You can't ignore these lessons. You need to learn these things, Mary. It's too important for you to pretend otherwise."

"But Augur..." I interrupt.

If looks could kill, I'd be done for. "She's so young," I say. "She's not going to be battling anyone."

"And you will be? You think you're strong enough to fight the disbelievers? You think you could battle with a disbeliever for more than one second?" He's practically spitting on my face.

"No, Augur, I don't think—"

"Then don't say idiotic things!" He turns back to Mary. I really wanted to point out that I never said that I could battle a disbeliever. I feel anger building up in my throat. Mary is still sobbing, just more quietly.

"Do you understand, Mary?" Augur says. She nods. "Tell me you understand, Mary. I need to hear you say it."

"I understand." Her voice is shaking. I try to put my arm back around her, but Augur pinches my hand hard, and I pull away.

"All right, class dismissed," says Uncle Dan. I get up and take Mary's hand. The look Augur gives me is withering, but I ignore him. That's the first time I've ever ignored him.

Outside, on the chapel steps, I let Mary run to the other little kids. I take a seat on the top step and drop my head into my hands. *What are you doing? You're already on thin ice. Why make things worse?*

Mary was miserable. How could I just sit there and let them fill her head with nightmares? *But you had those nightmares. You had that talk. You were told all the same stuff. And he's right. She can't pretend like it isn't going to happen. It is. It is.*

"Did you read the paper?" It's Uncle Dan's voice drifting out from inside the chapel. My ears perk up and I scoot closer to the window.

"Yes, Dan, who do you think is the first person to get the damn thing? Of course, I've read it," Augur responds with a hiss.

We get the paper?

"You really screwed up, Dan. You were supposed to be getting more discreet. What the hell is wrong with you?"

"But I thought you wanted me to—"

"I *wanted* you to make this end. I didn't want petty gossip starting. They think I'm hosting a nest of criminals."

"Well, I mean, you still haven't done anything about—"

"Watch your tongue."

"You know what? He's not even the problem. If anyone is a criminal, it's you. You've been fucking your sisters-in-law, your nieces and your stepdaughters, fucking *kids*—"

I hear the sound of a slap. Then a laugh.

"Oh, you want to fight, *Augur*?"

"No. I want you to do what you've been told. You'd do well to remember that I'm the one in charge here. And I've got everything under control."

"*Right*."

A rush of footsteps. In the nick of time, I scramble off the steps and behind the building. *Wham.* The chapel door flies open, and Uncle Dan stomps off.

When did we start getting the paper? Is someone writing about us? What is going on?

Overwhelmed, I take a deep breath. I hate this. I hate it here. I want to get out of here.

Calm down. You don't, really.

But I do. I want to leave. I need to leave. No one is going to protect me anymore. Summer has become someone I don't know. Sami...I've completely messed up everything with her. I have no idea if Augur is on our side anymore.

And I'm starting to wonder if God ever was.

PART TWO

Now

I 've never been on a bus before. It's incredible.

There are a lot of people jammed in here, knees bumping up against the seats in front of them, luggage stored in overhead containers (*if you're brave,* Lauren said) or under your feet (*if you're smart*). The bus driver isn't smoking, but he smells like he has been. In the seat across the aisle from me and Lauren, there's a couple who've been making out nonstop pretty much since we boarded. I think maybe they're running away together. The man in front of us has on the largest hat I've ever seen, a big, wide-brimmed brown felt thing. The woman behind us is knitting a lime green blanket. I've never seen such a variety of people in my life.

I'm actually enjoying it.

I still can't believe we haven't been caught yet. Lauren hasn't gotten a single call from her father, though I'm sure once breakfast passes and we're not there, he'll freak out and start calling every police station in the state.

Someone behind me keeps nervously tapping the back of my seat with their foot, but I'm too excited to care.

The bus engine rumbles to life, followed by a whooshing, wheezing sound, and then we're moving, turning out onto the main road, going past buildings that Lauren says are casinos and hotels.

I've never seen taller or shinier buildings. In fact, we almost missed our second bus because I spent so much time gawking once we got to Atlantic City.

Lauren counts our money again.

I'm starting to feel a bit drowsy, which makes sense. I've been awake since two in the morning, jittery with nerves.

"I never asked," Lauren says, turning to me. "Who is Samira Green?"

I tense up. Suddenly, the seat feels even smaller and more cramped.

"I just ask because you looked her up on my computer. Is she your relative or something?"

I laugh. Lauren frowns.

"What? You have the same last name."

"We all do," I say.

"Well, then, who was she?"

Who was Sami?

She was my best friend in the whole world. The only person who cared about me it felt like. She got mad when I got attention, but maybe only because she wanted to have me all for herself. The way I wanted to have her all to myself. She was the only person who ever understood me. Really understood me. She danced with me at weddings. Teased me. Drove me crazy with her insults and annoying jabs. And I cared about her with a desperation that made me feel like I was drowning. When we were together, it felt like we were meant to stay like that forever. I never wanted to let her go. And I never thought I would.

"Gracelyn?" Lauren snaps me out of it.

"She was... my friend."

"Oh." Her phone buzzes with a text. Her dad.

WHERE IS GRACELYN?!

Lauren Matilda Spicer what have you done?

WHY IS THERE A CHARGE FOR TWO BUS TICKETS TO CALIFORNIA ON MY CREDIT CARD?

"You used his credit card?"

"We didn't have enough for that and a motel!"

Lauren, just tell me you're okay.

LAUREN, YOU ANSWER ME RIGHT NOW. I WILL PERSONALLY MAKE SURE YOU NEVER USE THIS PHONE AGAIN IF YOU HAVE TAKEN YOUR MENTALLY UNSTABLE COUSIN TO CALIFORNIA WITHOUT MY PERMISSION.

"And so it begins," Lauren sighs.

"Am I mentally unstable?" I ask, reading the messages.

"I mean, kind of," says Lauren. We laugh. I never thought I'd be laughing at something like this, but here we are.

When the bus stops for the first time, we're told we have ten minutes before it leaves without us.

Lauren sets a timer for eight minutes and thirty seconds, and volunteers to stay with our stuff. "Head back the moment I text you. No one is being left behind at a rest stop. No one." The phone she's waving in my face buzzes with another text from the Tired Man.

I step off the bus. It's surprisingly nice to step out onto the cold concrete. I stretch, and my back cracks like an old woman's.

Inside the gas station, I look around hopelessly. I have no idea what she wants me to get.

Something catches my eye, though. Popcorn.

That was one of Uncle Dan's favorite things to get for us. I remember once he bought it instead of shoe polish for Augur's boots, and we didn't see him for two days. When he finally showed up at dinner, he had a black eye and looked like a ghost.

Focus. Get something sweet, too. I pick up some gummy worms and examine them. Radioactive looking, but fine.

I bring all the stuff to the counter, pay, then walk back to the bus. If I'm early, Lauren won't have to text at all. I still have no clue how to use this phone. It's an old one that Violet dug up from the back of her closet.

When I re-board the bus, Lauren looks so relieved I think she might just melt into a puddle. If she did, she'd be the least sticky thing on this floor.

"Oh, you got popcorn, nice."

"And gummy bears," I say, mildly upset that the other contribution hasn't been acknowledged. Lauren's phone buzzes again.

Lauren, I swear to God, if you don't respond in the next ten minutes, you are not going to have a social life, a phone or a computer for the next four years.

"He might a little upset," Lauren says, scrolling up to reveal about forty other messages.

She opens the bag of popcorn and digs a handful out.

"Hey, hey, you'll make a mess," I say. "We're gonna be sitting in this seat for the next three days. Please don't get that everywhere."

"Shorrry," she slurs through a full mouth.

I grab a handful of popcorn and allow myself to sit back.

I hope you know what you're doing.

Eleven Days Before

It's Christmas morning, and Aunt Gina and Uncle Oliver are gone.

Their clothing is gone, their belongings are gone. They've disappeared into thin air.

Maybe that's a bit of an exaggeration. I heard some people say that there are a few footprints near the gate.

Other than that, though, there's no proof they were ever here.

People have left before. Augur doesn't like to talk about it, but once he stopped letting us go to outside hospitals, a lot of people packed up and got out. The same thing happened when he started taking more wives and separating the men and women into different rooms. But of the people that remained after that, almost none have left. In fact, I don't think anyone has left since then, until last night.

I don't think we'll be celebrating.

We're all gathered in the dining room, eating oatmeal—or what passes for oatmeal. There's a lot of whispering going on. Gossip gets around fast here, although not fast enough for everyone to have heard before breakfast.

"What's going on?" asks Sami, sliding into the seat next to me. "Is everything okay?" We've moved past awkward silence and ignoring each other and now have short conversations. Awkward ones, but conversations, at least.

"Aunt Gina and Uncle Oliver left last night."

Sami raises an eyebrow. "What do you mean, *left*?"

"I mean left. Like adios. Like gone-in-the-middle-of-the-night-without-telling-anyone left."

"Seriously?"

"Seriously."

Her eyes widen. "Where do you think they went?"

"Does it matter? They're gone." I eat another spoonful of oatmeal. It's absolutely horrible. There's too much water at the bottom of the bowl and all the oats have made a dry lump in the middle that tastes like sand. But I'm starving.

"I mean, is anyone going to get them?"

"Why should they?"

"I don't know, Gracie. To get an explanation. What if they were, I don't know, government or something?" She slumps her head down toward the table. "God, I hate oatmeal."

"They weren't from the government. They probably just left so Aunt Gina wouldn't have to have a baby. Or maybe one of them got sick. They weren't government."

"You already said that," she replies, her voice muffled by the table.

"Jeez, was there a cockroach in your shower this morning?" I ask. "You're so moody." It's not a good joke. None of us has taken a shower in weeks, per Augur's orders, in order to lower our water bills.

"Sorry, I'm just tired." She props herself up on her elbows. "Has anyone seen Augur yet?"

I shake my head.

"He's gonna be mad." She says it like a joke, but I hear the worry in her voice.

"That's true."

I take my last bite of sand and wash it down with water. "One of his wives leaving? Oh yeah. He's going to lose his mind."

We all gather in the chapel, huddled together like penguins. It's surprisingly cold this morning. Augur stands at the lectern, face red, eyes ablaze.

Normally, I'd be up there next to him with Fawn and the other choir kids, singing Christmas tunes and looking forward to gingerbread cookies. But instead, I'm alone on a pew. Sami is with her parents. Fawn is in the back, far from everyone. And Summer's as close to Augur as she can be.

No one speaks. No one dares even move.

"My family," he starts, his tone somehow calm, despite the anger that I can clearly see on his face. "I'm sure that you all know what has happened today.

We have lost two members of our church to the disbelievers." He takes a deep breath. "Let this be an example to you all. Gina was my wife, and I gave her all the guidance and love that I could, but it was no use. Foolishly, I believed I could save her and her companion, Oliver."

Some people nod in acknowledgment.

"There are none among us immune to the devil's powers." He scans the room. "It could be Isaac. It could be his children—any one of them. It could be Glinda. It could be my dear Summer, or her sister, Gracelyn." I go bright red and feel my stomach churn.

"Gina was close to me. I thought her soul was capable of change, but I was wrong. If I was wrong about her, I could be wrong about any of you. Our lord forgives and saves, but some souls stubbornly defy redemption. Now, all of you must go about your work, but keep in mind that it is easier than you think to stray from the path of good and onto the path of evil."

My stomach keeps churning as we all get up and head for the door.

"Summer, Elizabeth, Hiram, Dan, could you stay behind, please?" Augur commands. Summer is in front of me, and I nearly walk into her back when she stops short.

She turns and joins the others gathered around Augur as he waits for the last of us to leave. For me to leave.

I close the door behind me and sit down on the steps. *That was intense.*

"Hey, ready to farm some carrots?" Sami stands over me, the sun creating a halo around her hair.

"Yeah. I guess."

"There is no guessing in carrot farming, Gracelyn, just facts—and carrots." She holds out her hand for me to take it.

"Jesus, okay." I grab her hand.

"Hey now, you're not allowed to take the lord's name in vain."

"Since when do you care about that?" I say, as we start walking toward the garden.

"Well, you know, ever since we were informed that any one of us could be a horrible, disgusting sinner, I've started to take all of our savior's rules much more seriously." Sami laughs as she says this, harder than I've heard her laugh in a little while.

That's when I know we're going to be okay—because Sami would never say something like that to anyone else. Honestly, I don't think anyone else would even let her *finish* a thought like that. But I always will. Always. No matter what.

Now

Our first night on the bus. Through tinted windows, the bright white headlights and blinking red taillights extend into the night like party streamers. Lauren insists she's nocturnal, so if I want to, I can sleep, and she'll nap during the day.

But falling asleep on a bus is hard. Especially when your mind is on fire. I try shutting my eyes and relaxing somehow, but I can't stop thinking about all that's happened, thinking about what we're doing here, thinking about what's going to happen next.

And then I'm standing in a ballroom that goes on for miles, wearing a dress that looks like the one I had at home, except without the rips or the dirt—it fits. My hair is long again. I'm not wearing any shoes.

No music is playing, but I have an incredible urge to dance.

I spin around, my skirt flaring out under me. I dance with an imaginary partner, taking careful steps around the infinite ballroom.

I see a figure in the distance. I stop dancing, and the figure steps closer. It's Sami. She's wearing a dress too, one that fits and looks soft. She's also barefoot.

"Would her ladyship care to dance?" she asks.

"It would be an honor, your highness." I put my hand in hers.

We dance, even though there's still no music.

"I missed you." She twirls me.

"I missed you, too," I say. "Not that this is real."

"Hey, I am extremely real."

"Well, yeah, but isn't this a dream?" I accidentally step on her foot.

"All right, fine, maybe you're not really seeing me. But isn't that what the trip is all about? Seeing me and Fawn, and all the others without it being tainted? Fixing everything and starting over?"

"Can I tell you a secret?"

"Always."

"This trip. It's just about you. It's only ever been you."

We go back to swaying back and forth.

"Why are you doing this?" She asks suddenly. "Why did you go back to how you were when we were little and just obeying everything he said?"

I swallow. She's right. I don't want to admit that, even to dream-Sami, but she is. "When I doubted things before, I always knew I'd have you. I knew that even if I had no other path, I had something else. But I lost all of that, and I just needed something to hold on to. I had to believe in something again, because if not, then I'd really have nothing." Everything is so blurry. "I needed it."

She stops dancing with me and holds my face delicately. "You don't need anything but yourself. You can doubt. It's going to help more than it will hurt."

"But I'm scared that he was right. I'm scared of how I felt about you. I'm scared of the end of the world."

"Everyone's scared of the end of the world." She smiles a little bit. "Normal people just ignore that feeling."

"We're not normal."

"Maybe we don't have to be." She leans back, trying to get away from me.

"Please."

"It's going to be okay. I promise."

I feel like I might die, but she smiles.

She pushes against my arms, and I drop her, and she falls out of my arms, towards the ground, which I just know is going to swallow her up.

I grab her arm before she hits the floor, pull her up and back into my arms, but suddenly her body becomes small. She's ten years old again, with a mouth stained orange. I step back. She tilts her head and looks at me questioningly.

"What's wrong Gracie?" Her ten-year-old voice echoes through the air. I take another step back and she grows into a twelve-year-old version of herself. "You're crying. That doesn't seem okay to me." She steps toward me. Her hair is short now. There are burn scars on her arms and hands. Tears in her eyes. She reaches out with one burned hand.

What happened to her?

My dress turns into a long white nightgown. My knees are scuffed, my fingers and arms have burn marks. My whole body is spattered with blood, I touch my hair and find that it's all been chopped off. The light is sucked from the ballroom, and the silence fills up with words and screams.

What happened to me?

Sami's hand is still held out to me. I reach out to take it because that's all I want. To be with again, to be safe. But the ground shakes under my feet. Something explodes with a loud pop.

"Hey, you okay?" Lauren touches my shoulder. "I think we drove over a bottle. Were you able to sleep?"

"You didn't notice?" I say, rubbing my eyes.

She lets go of my arm and laughs sheepishly. "Heh. I drifted off, myself, I guess."

"What time is it?"

"Four. You should go back to sleep."

"I think I'm okay." I don't want to go back into the infinite ballroom.

"You sure?"

I'm not sure of anything anymore. I'm not sure I know what's real, and what's not. I'm not sure what I believe in anymore—if I believe in anything.

"Yeah, I'm sure."

Ten Days Before

At breakfast, I gather enough courage to bug Summer about why she was in the chapel with Augur and the others all day yesterday.

The two of us hardly ever talk anymore. And the last time we did, she slapped me in the face. But today I'm too curious to stick to that.

"You were gone all day yesterday. What was that all about?"

"We were just talking. It's not important."

"For the whole day? Come on, Summer." I place my dish in the sink while giving her a sharp look.

"It's grown-up stuff, Grace. Don't worry about it."

"Grown-up stuff?"

She slams her hand down on the counter so hard I jump.

"Listen, young lady. I have everything under control, so why don't you keep your nose out of my business?"

The pain of being yelled at must show on my face because she immediately softens. "Hey, hey." She tucks a strand of hair behind my ear, then cups my cheek. "I'm sorry, baby girl. Augur had a project for me and Elizabeth and Dan and Hiram. It's really not all that interesting. I'm just tired, okay?" She kisses my forehead. "All right, now head out. You better warm up your voice."

She's right. I should leave her alone. I have Christmas songs to sing. I should forget this ever happened. I will.

But as I walk away, I keep replaying everything she said.

It's pretty much the longest conversation we've had since Jenifer was born.

And I don't believe a single word she said.

The energy in the chapel today is somber, even though everyone is doing their best to project holiday spirit.

As we sing "Glory to God" I look around, examining people's faces for clues. Something weird is going on. I can feel it.

Uncle Hiram stares hard at us singers, which is a bit off-putting, but nothing new. Aunt Elizabeth looks smug. She keeps staring at Augur as if she expects him to look back.

Glory to God in the highest
And on earth, peace to people of goodwill
We praise You
We bless You
We adore You
We glorify You

Uncle Dan looks scared, tired, and nervous. He plays with his fingers, the nails of which are bitten down to nubs. All of Summer's attention is on Augur, not on me or the rest of the girls, not on Jenifer, who seems on the verge of tears, but on Augur, as if he's the most amazing person in the world.

We give You thanks for Your great glory
Lord God, heavenly king
O God, almighty Father
Lord Jesus Christ
Only begotten Son
Lord God, Lamb of God
Son of the Father
You take away the sins of the world
Have mercy on us
You take away the sins of the world
Receive our prayer

And then there's Augur, who appears tired. Like he has the weight of the world on him. He doesn't look back at the women he's conspiring with, he doesn't look at us singers. He looks at the window, at his own reflection. It's strange, but seeing him do that, I suddenly realize something.

He doesn't care about us anymore. He's tired of this life, bored by the power, bored by the lies. I think he wants the apocalypse to come. He wants it to come because he's sick and tired of living this way. Maybe he thought it was coming a long time ago. And maybe, since the world won't end on its own, he's trying to *make* it happen.

In my bones, I know something is very wrong here.

> *Glory to God in the highest*
> *And on earth, peace to people of goodwill*
> *We praise You*
> *We bless You*
> *We adore You*
> *We glorify You*

Now

I get off the bus again for snacks. A supermarket called Piggly Wiggly.

Lauren says we're somewhere in New Mexico, which reminds me of where I once lived. It's dry and dusty, basically empty.

I wander down the fluorescent-lit aisles, looking at each neon package. I pick up a bag of chips and shake it. It's frighteningly red. Whatever, I'm starving.

I hum to myself while I'm in line for the checkout, but the lady behind the counter gives me such a dirty look that I walk out of the store in embarrassed silence.

Outside, leaning against the cement wall of the supermarket, is a short-haired woman in a leather jacket and shorts. An earring shines on her eyebrow; her jacket's a patchwork of phrase-laden buttons. She's smoking a cigarette. I must stare at her a little too long, because she notices and smirks. "Want one?" She takes a pack of cigarettes out of one of her jacket's many pockets and flips open the top.

I step closer and take one. I don't know why.

"You from around here, darlin'?" She takes a deep drag.

A simple question for anyone else. "It's complicated."

"Ah," she says, as if she understands completely. "The way you talk gives it away, though. You ain't from around here."

I should end this conversation.

"You must be looking for something."

"What?"

She drops her cigarette, then stomps it out under her boot. "If you're not from here, what are you here lookin' for?"

"Nothing here," I say, even though I shouldn't. "It's—well, she's—*they're* all in California."

"She, huh?" the woman smiles. "I hope you find her." She walks off, but not before turning back to say, "Enjoy the cigarette."

I walk back to the bus, blushing, unsettled. I shove the unlit cigarette deep into my pocket. I feel like I've been clocked.

Slumping down on the seat, I look over at Lauren, who has an odd expression on her face.

"What?" I open the bag of chips.

She hesitates, then reaches into her bag and pulls out a shoebox.

"This is yours."

I freeze. "What do you mean?"

"Before you got here they mailed us all this shit. Dad gave you your shoes and sweaters and stuff, but there were also all these photos. I wanted him to give it to you, but he didn't think you could handle it." She holds out a necklace, a delicate gold cross dangling off of an equally delicate silver chain. "This too." It's not mine. It's Fawn's, yet my heart beats fast, and I almost drop the chips on the ground.

Lauren shifts the top of the box, revealing a stack of photos that nearly spill over the edge. "I just wanted you to have them. I don't know if this is exactly the right time, but I didn't know when else to do it." The first one that catches my eye is of Summer and Augur, I think on their wedding day.

"Gracelyn? Are you okay?"

I feel sick.

I bolt out of my seat, heading toward the front of the bus. But as I fling myself out the steps, I miss one, and take a header, wiping out on the concrete sidewalk. My hands feel like I just slapped a wall, and they're kind of rough and bleeding a little.

Some lady bends down close to me. "Hon, are you okay?" Her accent is the same smooth southern drawl as Aunt Gina's. Which makes everything worse. She keeps asking questions. My ears are ringing. Pulsing waves in my head.

I'm hearing bullets and screams. Smelling fire.

"Mom. I want my mom," I say, mostly into the concrete.

Idiot. You don't have a mom. You don't have anyone.

"Where is your mom, honey? Is she here? Are you alone? Are you here with anyone?"

Lauren. "Lauren," I manage to squeak.

The lady starts yelling my cousin's name. Or maybe someone different starts yelling, I can't tell. There are many different pairs of shoes around me. People try to touch me, but I can't feel their hands. My brow is drenched in sweat and every time I close my eyes, I see a thousand tiny shards of my past. Shards I could barely remember before.

I see Lauren's black shiny boots. "Gracelyn? Are you okay?"

I don't know what to say. What is happening to me? Why can't I move? Why can't I see clearly? Why is everything rushing back now?

"Up, please?" *God, you sound like a toddler.*

Someone helps sit me up, and after a moment of silence, my heartbeat slows down, my hands start to steady, though they still burn. Someone cradles my head, and I let them. My vision clears a bit, the tears finally ceasing. I look at the people who are standing around me. A man offers me a scared smile. "You all right?"

I nod, though it's clearly not true.

There are whispers, questions. Lauren helps me stand and leads back toward the bus door. "Come on."

The man in the brown hat stands on the threshold, having a heated conversation with the driver, keeping him from closing the door. The driver looks concerned but not sympathetic.

We make our way past the driver, back to our seats, following the man in the brown hat. Someone says, "I think she's sick." "Or on drugs," someone else says. The bus rumbles back to life and pulls away from the curb. I curl up on my seat and close my eyes while Lauren puts the lid back on the box.

Sometime later, I emerge from another dream to see Lauren smiling at me and basically pretending nothing happened—which I'm beyond thankful for. We start a game of twenty questions. It's hard. I've seen so few movies or and barely read any books besides the Bible. But it's still kind of fun.

The next time we get off the bus, it's a few stops further along at a donut shop by a gas station. I've had donuts before, but I've never had one all to myself. I also try coffee. It tastes like dirt, but I like it. Coffee was another thing we weren't allowed to have, but after everything that's happened today,

I don't care much about following the rules. It's not like Augur will ever find out.

We still haven't talked about what happened.

And then we don't get the chance, because when the bus wheezes to a stop one more time, a blonde woman in very stylish clothes gets on, and Lauren lets out a little shriek.

"What's wrong?"

Lauren's blue eyes are nearly popping out of her skull.

"What?"

The blonde woman storms up the aisle toward us.

In the sorriest sounding voice I've ever heard, Lauren says, "Hi, Mom. How are you?"

"Oh my God, young lady! Do you have any idea? Do you have any idea of the upset and worry you've caused?"

"Have you met Gracelyn, Mom?" Lauren says in the same apologetic tone.

"As a matter of fact, I've been worried about both of you," her mother responds, looking at me and then immediately back at her daughter. "I mean for months I'm trying to figure out what's even going on with you and your father and this...cult business. And now you're running away?"

Lauren winces.

"And now you have the *audacity* to ask how I am? Let me tell you, Lauren Spicer, I am not okay. I am very not okay. And we are getting off this bus right now. Let's go."

"Mom, how did you even get here?" Lauren asks, sounding like she's got a mouthful of marbles, hardly daring to lift her head.

"I took a plane and then I rented a car, and I think you would do well not to ask any more questions. Unless you want to lose your phone in college, too. Get up, both of you."

"Dad isn't here, is he?" asks Lauren in a meek voice.

"No. Your father didn't know if I'd be able to get to you in time, so he flew out to California instead. A waste, since I'm bringing you back home right this minute."

"No!" Lauren is defiant.

Her mom gives her a withering look.

"I mean it. Gracelyn and I are not getting off this bus. We're staying."

"Lauren," her mother attempts a firm yet kind tone. "This is not a negotiation. I am the adult, and both your father and I are in agreement. You're going back to New Jersey immediately."

"But Dad's not even in New Jersey. He's in California. And that's where Gracelyn and I are going. You can't stop us."

"Oh, I sure as shit can."

Everyone on the bus has their necks craned and twisted around, staring at us. I can see the bus driver's eyes in his rearview mirror. But no one's saying anything. They're letting the free entertainment play out.

"I'm sorry, Mom," Lauren continues. "But Gracelyn and I are staying on this bus."

I'll admit, this woman is so scary, I'd do just about whatever she tells me to, but I can pretend that I'm brave if Lauren is going to keep up her bluff.

Pinching the bridge of her nose, Lauren's mom lets out a loud and frustrated sigh. "All right, Lauren, fine. If you want to stay here and explain this incident to your father, that's just fine with me. But we're calling him right now, and if he says you're going with me, *you will go with me*. And stay or go, you will be grounded for as long as you live in my house."

She nods toward the phone in Lauren's hand. Lauren dials what I assume is her father's number. He picks up almost immediately.

"Dad?" Lauren asks, as if she wasn't sure he would pick up. "Yeah, hi. Mom told me to call you. Yeah, she's here. Arizona, I think."

Satisfied, her mom backs down the aisle a bit, offering Lauren some privacy.

"Dad. Dad. Dad, please let me—" Lauren rakes a hand through her magenta hair. "Dad, I know. I'm sorry but could you please—" She groans quietly. "I don't have an attitude; you just won't let me talk!" Her voice reaches a fever pitch on the last word. There's a moment where I can't hear anything coming from her or the tinny speaker on her phone. "Sorry. I didn't mean to get angry. Just let me explain." She sighs loudly. "It's really complicated, Dad. I wouldn't just do this for no reason...no, Dad, this isn't about you and Mom. Not everything is about you and Mom. It's about *her*. Yes, Gracelyn, who else?"

Who else?

"No, I'm not *jealous*. God. I *am* helping her. She has another family, and they're in California. Hence the bus to California." She rolls her eyes. "That was a joke, Dad. No, it's not very funny." She gets quiet, maybe listening to him, maybe just thinking. "Dad, I am really, really sorry. I should have...I don't even know. I should have talked to you first, or something. But we didn't run away for kicks. Please let us get where we're going. We can talk about this more in California. That's all I want." Silence. "Okay. Okay. I'm sorry. Okay. I'll see you. Okay. Bye Dad. Thank you." She puts down her phone and looks over at her mom. "He says we can go. You can call and ask him if you want."

Her mom looks skeptical but seems to trust her. She takes out her own phone and begins texting. After a moment, she mumbles something like "for fuck's sake." And then stalks down the aisle. After a brief argument with the bus driver, she comes back, and picks up her purse.

"Apparently ticket holding customers are more important than the safety of two children." She leans down and gives her daughter a quick hug before grabbing her face forcefully. "I'm going to drive alongside you all the way to goddamn California, and Lauren, if you die on this bus, I swear to God I will murder you." As she walks off, she shouts behind her: "Let the record show that I am *not* happy about this. Your dad will be hearing from me."

She gets off the bus and walks to the car that's parked at the rest stop. I paste my face to the window and watch her get in, and rest her head on the steering wheel.

"Jesus *Christ*." Lauren slumps down in her seat and groans. The bus engine comes back to life, and a moment later we're on the move again. "That was the most stressful ten minutes of my life." She turns to look at me and smiles weakly. "On the bright side, we're more than two-thirds of the way there."

She breaks open the bag of chocolate candies we bought earlier and nervously fiddles one between her fingers. "Ugh. This is all falling apart."

She's not wrong. But we've gotten further than I ever thought we would.

I realize, as the sun starts setting, that I've seen more of the world in the past day and a half than I have in my whole life.

Ten Days Before

Sami and I just found whiskey.

We haven't hung out just the two of us much recently, but Augur canceled his sermon tonight, so we decided to sneak into the pantry. I don't think we've eaten anything but oatmeal and rice in a week, and Sami is feeling furious and reckless, so we decided to just go for it. We were looking for something to eat, but the only thing of interest is the whiskey. Sami kneels down and touches the brown bottle lightly.

"Wanna drink it?" She says this without any conviction.

I'm still in shock. "Uh. Where would we do that?"

"Right here." Sami motions to the dirt floor of the pantry.

"I don't know. This belongs to someone…"

"If it means that much to them, why'd they just leave it here? And it's not as if they can ask around or get mad. Then they'd have to admit they had it in the first place. Come on. We've got time until curfew. Everyone's asleep. Let's drink it." Before I can protest further, she pulls the cork under the loose white fabric of her shirt. It falls to the ground. She grins at me.

We are absolutely not allowed any drugs or alcohol, and as far as I know, no one our age has ever attempted to break that rule. But here we are.

I hesitantly step into the shade of the shed, and she takes a long swig from the bottle. When it finally leaves her lips, she sticks her tongue out. "Bleh." She holds it out to me. "It's awful."

I grab it from her. "That's encouraging."

It tastes like bitter apple juice and gives me an immediate burning sensation in my chest that makes me reach my arms reach up to the sky and let out a high-pitched squeal. Sami breaks into a huge, uncontrollable grin. Before we know it, we've polished off half the bottle and we're dizzy and giggling on the floor.

"Now I see why Augur doesn't allow this," Sami says, kicking her foot in the direction of the shelf where we found the bottle. "It would be too fun."

"Augur doesn't like us to do anything fun," I clarify. The words leave my mouth, seemingly without permission. "No whiskey, no love, no television except the stupid news. No books."

"Love?" Sami asks, sitting up slightly.

"Yeah," I backtrack quickly. "I mean, have you seen any happy couples that don't involve him lately? I haven't. Have you seen any romances? Have you seen—"

"I saw Allison and Kyle kissing the other day," Sami blurts out. "I promised I wouldn't tell but obviously that doesn't include you."

"Really?"

"Yeah, you're a good secret keeper."

"Not that, stupid. You really saw them kissing?"

"Uh-huh." Sami pauses for a moment to think. "You know, that was the first time I saw anyone kiss. Romantically that is."

"That can't be true."

"Augur never kisses his wives in front of us. They're the only ones allowed to touch, so I don't think so."

"Huh. Weird." I sit up and arch my back, stretching. "Was it gross?"

"No..." She looks up at the sky. "It looked nice. Like it meant something. She was happy, I could tell." Sami shakes her head like she's trying to throw the memory onto the ground. "Too bad I'll never know what that's like." She tosses back another few gulps of the whiskey. "You hear the rumors, don't you?"

"Which ones?"

She makes a face, lowering her gaze. "About Augur and his wives."

"I don't think so."

"Not about how they...you know."

"No, I don't know."

She shifts, uncomfortable. "Never mind. Never mind."

"You can't just say that and then not expect me to—"

"They all sleep together, Gracie. Is that what you want to hear?"

She picks up the bottle, which is now only a quarter full. She crosses one leg over the other and takes another sip of the whiskey.

"I don't understand."

"What's not to understand?" She still can't meet my gaze. "He makes them...do stuff together."

"Oh."

After a moment of uncomfortable silence, she says, "He's a hypocrite."

"What?"

"He's always going on and on about how homosexuality is a sin, but he still..." She blushes, bright red. "He's a hypocrite, that's all I'm saying."

The last time she talked about him like this was when we were on the roof almost two years ago. I wonder where that Sami has gone.

"So you think he's wrong?"

"Hm?"

"You think it isn't a sin?"

Her hair's tangled, oily and unruly. I can't think of the last time we were allowed to take showers with enough time to properly wash our hair. I can tell that she's embarrassed, because she's looking anywhere but at me.

"I don't know if I think anything is a sin." I notice her moving her hand closer to mine, slowly, maybe she doesn't even notice she's doing it. "I think there might just be actions. Nothing is holy, or unholy."

"That's a pretty unholy thing to say." I allow myself to edge my hand closer to hers.

She laughs, quietly. "Well, I guess I'm going to hell."

Our pinkies touch, interlock. I don't try to take more of her hand, and she doesn't try to take more of mine. But there is electricity in our minute contact.

And it's back. A desire to kiss her so intense it takes every ounce of my weakened will not to do it.

Somehow, I force my pinkie away from hers. Because keeping her safe is worth every impulse I have to bury; worth every word that's trapped under my tongue; worth every bit of myself that I'm hiding from the world; worth the way my heart aches when she looks at me; worth every moment I spend loving her in silence.

Because to me, going to hell doesn't feel like a joke.

"We should go back upstairs," I whisper.

"Yeah." She stands up and walks away, taking a drunken misstep and nearly falling over. I don't even have it in me to laugh. I just go over to her, shaky as I am myself, and prop her up.

Because that's what best friends do.

Now

"Are you sure you want to do this?" Lauren asks, hesitating to remove the box top.

I nod.

"Okay. Tell me if you get scared or triggered or whatever." She opens the box and starts sorting through the photos.

"I will." Darkness is settling in on the bus, and I'm feeling a little braver than I was in the daylight.

She takes out a few group pictures, of people sitting on the porch or working in the garden. They look older, like they were taken long before I was born. "I guess my biggest question is: what did you guys do all day in the middle of nowhere?"

I remember the daily schedule that appeared on the whiteboard in the main room every morning. I remember squeaky pink markers and groans of disappointment.

"We started doing little jobs when we were seven. And the workload increased as we got older. The work was mostly divided into jobs for men and jobs for women. The men handled all the dangerous and manual labor stuff like fixing our fence and gate—it got chewed up by animals all the time—and the women sewed clothes and gardened, stuff like that."

"But like, could you watch television, or read? Did you have games?" Lauren adjusts so her head is on the armrest.

"We could only watch one thing—the news—and that was usually on in the background of everything we did. We had one television, so there was no point in us sitting around it to watch. There were too many of us. Augur thought any other television was a waste of time."

Lauren looks horrified.

"We had a lot of copies of the Bible, but no other books, and the closest thing to a game we had were some playing cards. But no gambling."

"Was that like, bad? Did you mind that?" Lauren asks.

I pick photos up off her piles. "I mean, it wasn't the worst thing in the world. We had no reason to want that stuff. Eventually, we forgot..."

"Huh. Okay, moving on." She pulls out a photo of everyone at Bible study, and then another, and then another. "Jesus, how often did you do this?"

"A lot."

"Yikes," Lauren says.

I used to think it was something everyone should do, study the Bible so closely that you could quote full sections of it at a time. It felt so natural to be enthralled by interpreting scripture. But apparently, even people who love going to a normal church and who read the Bible in church and at home think that having Bible study for fourteen hours a week, every week for your whole life, is a bit strange.

We look at a few more group shots. I point out people I might have mentioned before, and try to pair each identification with a funny story, just to make it easier to swallow. Then we get to the wedding photos. There are a lot of them, and Lauren immediately notices a pattern.

"Who was the youngest girl that he married?"

I tense up, but I promised myself that I wasn't going to hide anything from her anymore. We came up with this plan that she was going to ask me questions about the photos and I was going to answer—and I feel like I have to honor it.

"I think..." I go through the list of his wives in my head, counting quietly on my fingers. "Aunt Haley was fourteen...maybe it was her? No, no. Aunt Deirdre was thirteen. But almost every girl was up for grabs. He could marry whomever he wanted."

Lauren looks very upset, but she shakes it off. "That's... *way* too young."

"Yeah, well." I'm not sure what else to say.

We're silent for a few minutes. Then she pipes up with, "Can you clear up the last name thing?"

Grateful for a change of subject, I launch into an explanation. "So, Augur thought that green was the color of most natural things, and since God created the natural, we should all be green, because that was the only way to be a natural creation of God. One day, Augur said that everyone had to refer to each other with the last name Green, and no one questioned it. There was no legal changing of our names, just the power of the collective." Even as I say it, I realize how ridiculous that sounds.

"Mmm...that's interesting?" She says it like a question. She examines a stack of photos, mostly of people working. "Did anyone have a real job?"

"No. I think before the false alarm some people did, but afterward, we lived off of people's inheritances and the money we made at gun shows."

"People just handed over their money?" she asks, wrinkling her nose.

"I mean, what else were they going to spend it on?"

She thinks about this for a second, then shrugs. "But what if they wanted to leave? Then what?"

I remember a girl with blonde pigtails came with her parents to check out the chapel one time. While they spoke with Summer and Uncle Dan, the girl asked me "what's the town nearby like? Do they have a candy store? I've never been to California," and when I told her, "No one ever leaves," she burst into tears and her parents took her home. I told Augur about this in confession, thinking I must have done something really wrong to make that girl cry, but he just laughed.

"Gracelyn, no one here will ever get in trouble for telling the truth."

What a load of shit that turned out to be.

Lauren takes my silence and reflection as a sign to push on. She flips over a photo in her hand. It's of a party. You can see Fawn and Juniper in the corner, playing pattycake or something.

"*Celebration after the false alarm*," she reads from the back. "What is that?"

"It was the first time the government came to inspect us. Nothing happened, no one got hurt. I was like seven."

"Oh." She turns the photo back over. "But what happened?

It's such a simple question, but it feels like a blow to the head.

Still. I did promise. "A group of government agents showed up at the compound, apparently to make sure nothing weird was going on. The adults wanted to get their guns and turn them away, but Augur told them all just to hide us kids away and let him handle it. Summer took me to the basement." I swallow. "All the other young kids were there, and we all had to sit in that basement room together, in the dark, for the whole day. No one came back for us until like, three a.m., and by then we were all starving, crying, and most of us had peed on the floor, because we had no other choice.

"When the adults came back for us, they didn't apologize or explain themselves. They just got us all changed, gave us some food, and put us to bed. I remember crying myself to sleep that night with all the other kids..." Lauren looks shocked, but I can't stop. The words keep spilling out.

"Augur sweet-talked them just like he said he would, told them that it was just him and his extended family living there. They wanted to know about guns. He said that they only had three, just for protection and hunting. Then they asked him if they could look around. He told them, sure, and when they did, they found more than three guns, but since none of them were illegal, they went away.

"Of course, it was all lies. Augur was only related to *his* kids, and we must have had hundreds of guns, a lot of them illegal—not that Augur cared about the law." I stop there, pressing my head into the back of the seat.

"Wow..." Lauren pauses, looking thoughtful. "Why did they put you in the basement? What did they think would happen if the government had seen you all?"

"Well," I snap. "What happened the second time they came to *look around,* Lauren?"

"I'm sorry, I didn't mean to--"

I breathe deeply. *Calm down.* "You don't need to apologize. *You* didn't do anything."

"Yeah, I just can't believe you had to go through all of that."

I look at my shoes. "I'm sorry if you get in trouble from all of this."

Lauren laughs, seeming relieved at the subject change. "This was my idea, remember. Plus, this is the most exciting thing I've ever done! I said that before we even left."

"Yeah, you did."

"Okay, more questions..." She picks up the stack I've been avoiding, the one with all the photos of us kids, but then puts them down and looks at me. "This is a bit more of a personal one, but was there ever any kind of romance? Between anyone except the guy and his wives I mean."

It's somehow weirder to hear her call him "the guy," than it is hearing people use his real name. "Um, other people were allowed to get married. No one was allowed to have kids, but women and men slept in different quarters, so it didn't even really matter. The marriages were pointless, because everyone was kept separate, and Augur could marry anyone, even if she was married to someone else."

"I can't believe people put up with that," Lauren says, shaking her head in disbelief. "What about the younger people? Kids get crushes, right?"

"Well, there was Kyle and Allison. They seemed to really like each other." I reluctantly pick up the pile and look for a photo of the two. Sure enough, Kyle and Allison sitting on the porch fence, almost falling off and laughing. I hand it to Lauren, who grins. "But she's dead now, so it doesn't matter."

Lauren's face falls. "Oh my god. I totally forgot. I'm so stupid."

"You're not stupid. You had no way of knowing."

After a moment, she gets a mischievous glimmer in her eye. "Did you ever have a crush on anyone?" She raises an eyebrow.

Kids get crushes. Right?

"Um..." I blush. "I-I don't—I don't think—" I stutter.

"Oh my god, you totally did. Tell me. Come on..." Her face goes from suggestive to ashamed within two seconds. "Oh, no, is he dead? I—"

"No, not dead. Just..." *You can't seriously be about to tell her.* "We were friends, and I didn't realize it might be something more for a long time. And then..." *And then you realized it wasn't just a crush. You got overwhelmed and said stuff you regret now. And then you two fell apart and your home burned to the ground.*

"And then everything went to hell."

"Who was it?" Her voice is quiet, but full of curiosity.

Go on. You've told her this much. Why don't you admit your sins to her—to the world?

Before I can say anything, she lets me off the hook. Maybe she senses she's pushing too hard. "It doesn't matter," she says. "Can I ask you one more question?"

I shrug. "Okay. But then can we move on?"

She nods vigorously. "Were you in love?"

My heart stops.

"I mean, we're really young still, but that sounds like the most amazing and tragic love story ever." She tilts her head, eyes misting over. "Were you?"

"I—" *You promised.* "Yeah. I was in love." I pick up the photos, sift through, and find the one I knew would be there. The one I pinned to my wall above my bed. Of me and Sami in our tattered dresses, sitting on her bed before a wedding, grinning at the camera. I force myself to hand over the picture, and I stop breathing, waiting for what I know is coming.

"Her?" Lauren says. "Wow. I'd watch the shit out of that movie."

I blink, shocked. "Wait—you're not... mad? You're not upset with me?"

"Why would I be upset?" She goes right back to looking through the box.

"I don't know... I just—"

"What?... You're the same person you've always been to me."

I almost burst into tears. I reach over to hug my cousin, and even though she's bewildered, she hugs me back.

Eight Days Before

Augur's sermon ended three hours ago. Now it's five in the morning, and I still haven't gotten to sleep.

I know that Sami's awake, too. I can hear her tapping on her bed frame, which she does all the time. It's annoyingly loud. I don't know how Vera, her bunkmate, hasn't strangled her yet.

The sky outside the window is still dark. Technically, we're not allowed to leave our rooms at night, but I don't think I'm going to sleep anytime soon. I quietly hop out of bed and grab my guitar from the closet. I may as well get some practice in.

I'm almost sure Sami sees me leaving, but she doesn't say anything.

Augur gave me a few more songs to learn. He decided I needed some love songs, since there are more weddings coming up. I'm excited for the next one—I'm perfecting one song in particular.

I play it from the beginning. It's difficult even though the melody is pretty simple. Fact is, it's probably the hardest song I've tried to learn yet. I sing,

"*Wise men say, only fools rush in.*"

The notes are all wrong. I drop my guitar and it bangs against on the porch steps.

Jesus, everything is going wrong.

Footsteps.

Please don't let it be Augur or Summer or any other adult. Please, just give me a few seconds to think, to clear my head.

"Hey." It's Sami. She's leaning against the doorframe. "Can't sleep?"

"Is it that obvious?"

She smiles.

I pick up the guitar again and try to act nonchalant. She comes over, sits down next to me, drums her fingers on the porch.

"I used to be so jealous of you."

"Really?" It's weird to hear her admit it even though I already knew.

"You have this talent that everyone appreciates, everyone gets to experience. And with Augur, it's not just something you share with him, it's almost like he gets a kick out of seeing how jealous it makes me." She takes a deep breath, looks down at her feet. "Even so, I could listen to you play for hours. I love listening to you play." She looks up again, directly into my eyes. "Or maybe it's that I just can't stay mad at you."

I blush and look away, focusing on my guitar.

"Wise men say, only fools rush in.

But I can't help falling in love with you."

I sneak a quick glance. Now, Sami's the one blushing.

"Shall I stay?

Would it be a sin?

If I can't help falling in love with you?"

"Don't stop," she whispers, looking almost teary.

I stop anyway. I desperately want words to come out, but nothing will.

"I really, really wish I knew what you were thinking right now," Sami says, filling the silence. "Because either you know what I'm trying to say, or you don't."

I know what she's trying to say. I just don't know how to respond. Sami shivers in the night air. "It's funny," she says with half a laugh. "I understand so little of what happens in your head. And I spend *so* much time trying to figure it out. I used to think—no, I used to be sure—that you felt the same way I did. But these days, I think you might just be full of crap."

"Excuse me?"

"I know you're not actually that stupid. You're smarter than me in a lot of ways. You're a fucking good actress, you know that?"

I recoil. "What is wrong with you?"

"Everything." She presses the heels of her hands into her eyes. "God, you're a moron."

"I have no idea what you're talking about. And you're talking really loud. Someone's gonna wake up."

"Who cares? Everyone's just waiting for the end of the world. They don't give a shit what we do."

"You know that's not true."

"We could do this. If we really, really wanted to, we could. It would be so easy to hide. No one would ever know."

It's not like I don't know exactly what she's talking about. I'm not that dense. It's not like I haven't imagined over and over what it would be like to admit how I feel about her. To hold hands under the table at dinner, to kiss during moments like this at night. To keep dancing at weddings and in empty rooms. It's not like I haven't felt euphoric imagining these things.

But then I imagine us dragging each other through the desert after being exiled, or begging for our lives in the chapel, or dying of dehydration in the basement. And the euphoria stops.

"It's just that it's so dangerous."

"Am I not worth it?" She's trying for lightness, but I can tell she's hurt.

"Come on. We both know that's not it."

"What then?"

"You aren't scared at all?"

"Of course I am," she whispers, taking my hand. "What about *you*?"

I look at her big, starlight-filled eyes. "Of course I am."

I see the regret and fear flash across her face, but despite it, she inches forward. She moves her head, moves it back, and despite myself, I smile. "Are you going to do it?"

"Shut up," she says, and then she kisses me.

After a moment of shock, I kiss her back, giddy, nearly lightheaded with happiness. It's not a perfect kiss—my teeth knock against hers, our noses touch. But it feels magical, the most terrifying and beautiful thing that's ever happened to me.

My whole life, I've been glad I wasn't born outside, where the disbelievers could corrupt me. I detested the idea of a normal life. But good lord. Right now, I would do anything to be sitting on the bleachers of a normal high-school, in a cheerleader uniform, sitting next to Sami, not worried about being killed, or about the end of the world. I would do anything for a life like that.

"This isn't going to end well," I say when we pull apart.

"I know," she says, kissing me again. "But let's pretend for a second that it will."

Now

We've arrived.

When we finally stagger off the bus on shaky legs, it's into a crowded California bus station. Before we even take our bags out of the bus's compartment, Lauren gasps. She's spotted the Tired Man. He's running toward us, pushing people aside.

For a split second, I think he's going to hit us, but instead, he wraps us both in a hug. For the first time ever, I don't flinch away from him. "Thank God you two are okay." He leans back to get a better look at us. We must look like a total mess. We're unbathed, hungry, and tired. "Never, *ever* do that again," he adds, pulling us both back into his arms.

"Hey, Dad," Lauren says, her voice emotional. She looks really happy to see him. Surprising, since she enjoyed running away from him so much.

"Your mom is stuck in traffic. She'll see us later. And I had a whole angry speech planned, but I'm just so glad that you aren't hurt that it'll have to wait," he says, releasing us from his embrace. "Let's get some real food in you, and maybe after that, we'll discuss what happened."

An hour later, our "discussion" gets so heated that other patrons at the diner turn to see if we're okay.

"Seriously, what were you thinking?" the Tired Man roars, his face turning red. "Taking a *bus* to California? Are you two out of your goddamn minds?"

Lauren seems like she's about to say something, but then thinks better of it, which is probably a good thing.

"What did you think would happen?" the Tired Man says. "Did you really think I wouldn't take you straight home? Because that's what's happening, girls. I'm taking you right back to our side of the country, and I'm taking you the second the waiter brings our check!"

The couple next to us whisper to each other. I blush, slightly humiliated.

"Dad, please. We made it this far. You have to let her see her friends," Lauren begs.

Not my friends, I think. *My family.*

"Oh no, oh no. I am not doing anything to interfere with Gracelyn's progress, and I am certainly not going to let you stay here for three more seconds!" He takes a furious bite of his pancakes.

"But Dad—" Lauren ignores the deadly look he gives her. "She's made so much progress on this trip. She let me ask her questions, and she talked—a lot. Please."

"Lauren, we're going home. End of discussion." The Tired Man tries to flag down a very timid teenage server, who pretends not to see him and ducks into the kitchen.

"Dad, can we talk over there?"

"Lauren, are you listening to me?"

"Yes! Just… can we please talk in private?"

"Fine." He stands up and drops the napkin on the table dramatically. Lauren shoots me a look as they head toward the bathrooms.

"Good luck," I mouth.

I feel beyond cowardly having Lauren fight this battle for me. To ignore that cowardly feeling, I take a bite of my omelet. It's not fantastic, but I'm so excited for any kind of real food that I start shoveling it into my mouth. When I finally stop to catch my breath, I look over to see how the argument is going. Lauren is pointing in my direction, trying to make some sort of point. The Tired Man tugs at his ear in frustration.

I'm feeling cowardly but also impatient. I'm just a few miles away from my family, and yet here I am, eating an omelet and waiting for my uncle to stop freaking out. I need to speed this along somehow. Or Lauren does.

By the time they come back inside, I've cleaned my plate. The Tired Man takes a deep breath and sits down. He places his hands, which are balled up into fists, on the table. "Okay." He clenches his eyes shut. "Okay. Look. We are going to a hotel. You two are going to get a full night's sleep and a shower. I will deal with your mom. And then in the morning, we are coming back to this diner, and then we are driving to the Abraham Maslow psychiatric facility. You're getting your time with your friends and family. And *then* we are going home."

My eyes must look like they've doubled in size.

"Thank you, thank you, thank you!" This is Lauren, speaking for me again because I can hardly move, I'm so shocked. The Tired Man flags down a server.

"What did you say to him?" I mouth.

She smiles mischievously and whispers in my ear. "I told him there was someone special you needed to see."

We check into the Dixie Hollywood hotel, a brightly colorful bungalow-style place with a mural of palm trees and the Hollywood sign in our room. Lauren takes a shower, then almost immediately passes out on the bed we're supposed to share. I sit at the foot brushing my short, wet hair.

The Tired Man leans against some pillows on the other bed, watching sports on the TV.

"I'm sorry," I say.

He mutes the TV and looks at me quizzically.

"For running away. For taking Lauren with me. For not telling you. For lying. Lying, like a lot. Guilting you into staying and not actually even doing the guilting myself. For not wanting to get better when I was with you." I feel tears well up in my eyes. "I'm sorry for being mean. For running away that one time from Dr. Yen, and for all the pain I've caused you. For reminding you of my mom. And not obeying you."

His face softens. "Oh, Gracelyn." He motions for me to come over. He puts an arm over my shoulders. "I'm not mad at you, and you don't have to apologize. For any of it. I only wish I could make all this go away for you. I wish I could take away all the hurt in your life." He hugs me even tighter.

There's still a part of my brain that tells me not to trust him, and yet, right now, in his arms, I feel safe, safer than I've felt in a very long time.

He loosens his grip on me and sighs. "I know you don't remember her, but your mom, she was kind of electric. She was vibrant and brilliant, and though we were different in a lot of ways, I was always in awe of her. I never thought my older sister would get caught up in something like that. It's a side of her I guess I'll never really understand." He rubs his eyes. "But I'll never forgive myself for not trying to get you and your sister out of there as soon as I could."

We grow silent. All I can hear is the quiet rumble of the ice machine.

"Did you ever meet Summer?" I ask.

"I looked after her for a bit when you were born. She seemed like a sweet, smart kid. I hate to think that bastard came along and ruined her."

"She was like that once," I say. "Smart and sweet, I mean. But for most of my life, she was just...I don't know...bitter? Jealous? Sometimes it felt like she didn't love anyone or anything other than him. I know she was willing to kill and die for him. She took care of me, but I wound up hating her—not that she seemed to notice." I take a shaky breath. "No, that's not true. I didn't hate her. I loved her. I tried to help her, but she just hurt and ignored me, over and over and over."

"You don't think she loved you?"

I ponder that for a moment and eventually settle on: "I don't think she felt much at all."

He presses his lips together like he understands.

"It's not like I was the only one who was starting to question things," I say. "But as far as I know, she never did. She died thinking she was married to God, and she was going to heaven."

"You don't think that's what happens?" he asks gently.

"I don't think she went anywhere. I think she just died."

He laughs. "Spoken like a true agnostic."

"Excuse me?"

"It's—never mind."

We sit in silence for a moment. I reach over and put my hand awkwardly on top of his.

"Thanks for everything, Nathan."

"Don't mention it, kid. Now let's get some sleep. We've got a big day tomorrow."

EIGHT DAYS BEFORE

Sami kisses me again and again; and a few times, I kiss her. There's definitely a learning curve. But I think we're getting the hang of it.

She examines my face and brushes a strand of hair behind my ear. "Can I ask you something insane?"

"Yeah, of course," I say breathlessly.

She takes a deep breath before mumbling, "What if we left?"

What?

"Gracie?"

"You can't say things like that, Sami. It's... there's no point. We can't leave."

"Aunt Gina left."

"And? Who knows what they're doing to her out there? She's probably getting tortured right now."

"Oh, shut up. You don't actually believe that bullshit anymore, do you?"

"Sami, Stop." Sami pulls away from me and crosses her arms.

"What's wrong with you? Why are you freaking out?"

"We shouldn't even be doing this. It's sinful. It's wrong."

"What?" She looks like I just slapped her.

"Augur has always told us it's wrong. Only men and women should be together." I can't believe what's coming out of my mouth, but I can't stop it. "We have to stop, Sami. Before it's too late. You're already talking about *leaving*. We're becoming sinners. Disbelievers."

She scoffs. "Bullshit."

"You know it's true. Our friendship has always been way too intense. It's unhealthy. We should have stopped being around each other a long time ago."

"Says who?"

"Summer. She always said you were too possessive of me."

"Well, fuck Summer!" Sami grabs my hands. "Who cares what your sister thinks? This—" she motions between us, "—is too real to let go because of *her*."

"But it's *not* real." I drop Sami's hands. "Augur always said—"

"We were just talking about how he's a hypocrite! He doesn't actually believe it, Gracie. He just *says* things he thinks people will agree with. He's no authority!"

"Yes he is, Sami! He's the authority on everything. He speaks to God!"

"You honestly still believe that?"

"Yes."

The word comes out of my mouth so quickly. A reflex, maybe. But somewhere in my head, I believe it. No matter how illogical it is. No matter how much hurt is on her face right now. I can't stop believing in him just like that.

Sami's eyes fill with tears. "I thought you were smarter than that," she says. "I thought you cared about me."

"I do—" I say, but I can tell it's not enough. I feel like I've just ruined our perfect moment. The one good thing I had in this whole world, and I've ruined it. *Fuck.*

"You're right, Gracie. I'm a disbeliever. I'm exactly the kind of person Augur warned you about. But you know what?" Angry smirk, tears still running down her face. "Whatever I am, you are too. You're a sinner and a homosexual and a fucking traitor to your sister and Augur and everyone in this place. You can't take that back. So I hope giving me up was worth it." She gets to her feet. "Believing in him can't make that not true." She turns away.

I grab her arm. "Sami..."

"Let go of me."

"No—"

"Gracelyn. Let go." Hearing her say my full name breaks my heart. So I let go.

That's when we both hear it—the compound pickup truck rolling down the road in our direction, dust dancing in its headlights. I hadn't even realized that it was gone. I feel a pit in my stomach.

"Shit."

"I'm going inside," Sami says. "If they see us together, we're fucked."

"Hey..." There's so much more I want to say. "You know I didn't mean any of that, right?"

She sighs, opening the door and looking back at me one more time before heading in, dragging my heart with her.

The pickup grinds to a halt, and I duck around the side of the porch, crouching behind a rain barrel. I can see my sister and Uncle Hiram get out of the car, and then Aunt Elizabeth and Uncle Dan slide out of the backseat. They're arguing about something. All of them are covered in what looks like mud.

"Summer, you shouldn't really be talking about who made mistakes tonight," says Aunt Elizabeth, stomping toward the porch.

"I'm not the one who forgot to bring her gun."

"Girls, this isn't helping. Let's get cleaned up and try to get a little sleep," says Uncle Hiram, face stoic and unfeeling.

"Hiram is right. And let's try not to make a mess inside, too," Uncle Dan says.

They all stomp noisily through the door, still grumbling at one another, so wrapped up in whatever's going on with them that they walk right by me. I can hear them still through the open window. I stay where I am, listening, not daring to breathe.

"I can't believe you kept that stupid thing," says Summer, voice full of spite.

"He wants proof, doesn't he?" says Aunt Elizabeth.

"Whatever." A pause. "Leave it on the mantle."

I hear the faucet running. Vigorous scrubbing. And then, after the water's turned off, footsteps retreating down the hallway.

I come out from behind the barrel, relief washing over me because they obviously didn't see me or Sami.

Inside, I step quietly over to the sinks. They're still wet and puddled. One of the white handles has a spidery brownish handprint on it. I look closer and feel a shiver. *Blood.*

A floorboard creaks behind me. I whirl around and see a shadow disappear into the hallway. My heart leaps in my chest, but my curiosity is too strong.

I go over to the mantle to look at Aunt Elizabeth's "proof."

It's a hair clip. A flower-shaped hair clip like the one Aunt Gina always wore. It's too dark to tell what color it is, but I'm pretty sure it's Aunt Gina's.

It's covered in dark fingerprints.

"Oh Summer," I whisper to myself. "What have you done?"

Now

"Are you ready?" asks Lauren.

I take a deep breath and look at the looming glass building in front of us. "No. But I'm doing it anyway." I stuff my hand in my pocket to make sure the paper is still there. It sits next to the cigarette from the gas station lady.

"All right, well, we'll be right there if you need us." Lauren squeezes my hand. Nathan nods in affirmation.

The woman who was at the reception desk when I left this place the first time (what seems like a lifetime ago) is still here. I don't know if she remembers me, but even if she doesn't, she offers a kind smile while giving us our instructions. We're required to leave before five but we can see as many patients as we want while we're here. She warns us that the people here have experienced a lot of trauma, and I nearly laugh because I know more about their trauma than she ever will. Nevertheless, I promise to be respectful and understanding of everyone's boundaries.

"Fawn wants to talk with you alone before you visit all the others. Her room is just through here." I follow the receptionist down a hallway, leaving Nathan and Lauren in the lobby. The receptionist knocks on a door, then opens it.

"Fawn? You have a visitor."

Through the open door, I see Fawn for the first time in months. A burn mark stretches from her left temple to her chin. When I saw a photo of Uncle Jim on the news, there was a massive burn on his arm, so I knew some of the other survivors would be scarred this way. Even so, seeing it is rough.

She's wearing a headscarf, and I wonder if that's because her hair got burned off. She had the most beautiful hair, long, thick and dark. I used to brush it for her, and Sami would weave little braids into it. She runs up and throws her arms around me. "Gracie!"

I hug her back. She's trembling.

"I missed you so much," she says, her voice choking.

"Are you okay?" I ask after the receptionist leaves. It's hard to know if Fawn was being honest during our phone call.

She releases her grip on me, though we keep holding each other's hands. "I'm okay. I actually like it here. It seems like maybe some of us are getting better." Despite the burn scars, there's more meat on her bones. Her face is rounder, healthier. Her eyes look a little hollow, but not completely void of life.

"Better how?"

Fawn laughs. "I don't even really know what I mean by that. But the kids are drawing nice, normal things instead of... apocalyptic things. I've stopped having bad dreams every single night. This..." She indicates her face. "...has started healing." She takes a deep breath. "I don't know, Gracie. I just *feel* better."

"I'm so glad, Fawn," I say, doing everything in my power not to stare at her burn. "But what's going to happen to the orphans? Have they said?"

"Some of them have family like you and Juniper. Some of the families only just found out that us kids even existed. The rest are going into this thing, 'foster care,' where people take in kids who have no family or parents. So basically everyone has somewhere to go."

"What about you and Kyle and the older kids? What about Eve and Dawn?"

"Kyle will be a legal adult in a month. So, he can leave, lead his own life. You know Kyle, he never likes to talk about himself, so I have no idea if he has family. I think he already had a plan to run away with Allison, so maybe he has a house figured out or something. I don't know. Did you know she had asthma? That's why she went so quickly. No one ever knew." She's twisting her fingers together.

"What about *you*, Fawn?"

She sighs and looks up at a spot on the ceiling. "I'm not sure what I'm going to do. They're trying to track down my parents. I don't even know if they're still alive. Or maybe they just don't want anything to do with me anymore." She blinks a few times, obviously trying to hold back tears. "Eve and Dawn are fine. In the dark about what's going on with the trials. Uncle Jim might go to jail, but not for long enough to affect their lives. They might even be here until he gets out. But I don't know."

"Fawn, I'm sure your parents care about you," I say, putting my hand on her arm. "They'll probably hear about you when you go on TV for the trials. They're going to be proud of you."

"Gracie, I'm not…" She takes a deep breath, flinching. "I'm not going to do the trial."

"What? Fawn, I thought you wanted to—"

"I did. But I can't. I can't look into his stupid beady eyes, and I can't listen to him defend what he did to me. I'm just not strong enough, Gracie. I can't do it. I'm stronger in so many ways now, but I just can't do it." She starts crying. "I'm sorry. I'm sorry."

I'm stronger too. I'm better too. But I know there are still things that are too hard. I know, I know.

"Fawn, you don't have to apologize. If you can't do it, you don't have to. You've been through so much already, with Hiram and… the baby. You shouldn't have to do anything else you don't want to."

"Yeah." She wipes her eyes.

We stand there, awkwardly, silent for a moment.

"It started so slowly," she says suddenly.

"What?"

"It started with the compliments. And the staring. I remember, one time we were farming, and he said it was amazing that my hands were so soft, since I I was always digging in the ground. I wondered how he knew how soft my hands were." She smiles half-heartedly. "So, I asked him how he knew, and he just grabbed my hand and I let him. I didn't realize what was happening, so I just let him." She takes a shaky breath. "At first, I really thought he loved me. I thought he was trying to act like my dad, since I didn't have one anymore. But then he started complimenting my body.

"The first time it happened, it was at night. I was half asleep. And it…" She stops and takes a deep breath. "I tried to pretend nothing was happening and ignore what was really going on. But part of the reason it hurt is that I was mad. All his compliments, the idea that he valued me as a person, were bullshit. God, I hated him for that. But I will not let him ruin my life, Gracie. I won't."

I don't say anything. I just hug her. I hate him as much as she does. But she doesn't need hate right now. She needs love. Real love. She needs someone to hold her tight and tell her everything's okay.

So that's what I do.

Jenifer leaps into my arms the second I open the door to what Fawn tells me is the "Group Therapy" room.

I'm not even sure if my niece recognizes me. She's only two. Either way, she seems excited to see me. "Jenifer!" I'm worried I might crush her, I wrap her so tight in my arms. I don't know if she'll ever really understand what's going on now or what happened to her, but she seems okay.

All the other kids start crowding around me. I kneel, still holding tight to my niece, but I try to gather as many of the other little ones in my arms as I can. They all talk over each other and push to get close to me.

"I missed you all so much," I say.

"We missed you too," says Eve. "What took you so long?" Even though she's clinging to my left shoulder like a toddler and wearing a glittery pink headband, she sounds so mature.

Her twin sister, Dawn, chimes in, "Yeah, what took you so long?"

"Sorry guys," I say. "I kinda got held up."

"We forgive you," Dawn says, taking me literally.

I bite back a laugh. "Much appreciated. How are you guys, anyway?"

They keep talking over each other, voices and stories overlapping, but somehow, I'm mostly able to follow them. Even Vera looks excited to see me. I offer her a hug, and she accepts it.

"Are you staying? Are you staying?" Yotam asks.

Before I can answer him, the door squeaks open. And we all turn our heads.

"Hey Sami," one of the kids says.

January Fifth

Someone is shaking me awake.

"Get up, get up, get up." Fawn pulls and pushes on my arm as if it's a stubbornly stuck door. "Goddamn it, Gracelyn, get out of bed."

"Fawn? what's going on?" I lift my head and blink and rub the sleep from my eyes. She looks panicked.

"It's happening Gracelyn. It's happening. They're here. Get out of bed."

"What's happening? Who's here?" I ask, even though I know.

"Don't be stupid, there's no time. We have to get the kids to the basement, let's go." She pulls harder on my arm, dragging me from bed. "Come on!"

I stagger behind her into the main room. The moment I look out the window, I see the helicopters and government trucks in the distance. *This is happening. Oh God, it really is.*

The others are standing to the sides of the windows, holding guns at the ready. No one's shooting yet, but the sight of the guns alone is terrifying. Uncle Hiram thrusts a rifle at me with his big, meaty paw. I have no choice but to take it.

He shoves a gun at Fawn, too. Hers is bigger, and she nearly drops it.

"Don't kill each other," he says. There's a huge chest full of ammunition on the far side of the room, and some of the others are loading up or stuffing extra bullets in their pockets.

From the looks of it, there's enough ammo in that chest to kill every one of us three times over. I'm about to load up my pockets like everyone else when

I realize that I'm still in my nightgown. That's when Fawn starts dragging me toward the basement door to help the little kids down the stairs.

"Hurry up," I beg, my heart thumping, hands so slick with sweat I can hardly hold my weapon. Overhead, the deafening chuff of helicopter blades.

"I'm going as fast as I can," she grumbles, helping Abraham through the door.

"But Fawn, look." I point at the window.

Tanks crush our fence under their wheels. The fence that we've worked on for years, just gone. There are trucks behind them, and at least two dozen government agents with assault weapons. We outnumber them in terms of bodies, but the tanks and the sounds of their helicopters are terrifying.

Fawn and the others get the last of the kids downstairs and shut the basement door. Aunt Elizabeth and Uncle Jim run back up to the second floor. Others head to rooms down the hall, but most of us take up positions by the windows, clutching our guns. I see looks on faces ranging from terror to glee.

Augur marches into the room like a star taking center stage. He's wearing jeans, a button-down shirt and cowboy boots. His hair is pulled back in a ponytail, almost as if he's been grooming himself this whole time. He calmly walks over to the door, gives a meaningful nod to Uncle Hiram and Uncle Holden, then pulls the door open and, with them following him, struts out onto the porch.

A booming voice shakes the walls. "This is John Helicon of the ATF. We have a warrant for the arrest of Randolph Milly, Summer Alverb, Elizabeth Gilford, Hiram Johnson, and Daniel Nakamura."

Uncle Hiram and Augur are already out there on the porch. I don't see any of the others. The same thought I had the other day burns through my head. *Summer, what the hell did you do?*

I can hear Augur's response faintly from outside. "Well, you've got two of us right here. Can I help you with something?"

Suddenly, a shot.

I don't know where it comes from. All I know is that I hear it, distinct and clear, and whether it was us or them doesn't really matter, not now. All that matters is that it unleashes Armageddon, a deafening torrent of gunfire.

Shots start ripping through the windows and walls into the building. I dive to the floor. Other, braver people, by the windows, start firing back. My ribs ache where they smashed into the floor. Someone whispers a prayer practically into my ear. I can hear bullets zinging overhead, loud popping here in the room and from upstairs, too.

Suddenly, there's a misting spray of blood, and Aunt Deirdre falls to the ground. I scramble to see if she needs help, but one look at the gaping bloody hole in her skull and I know there's nothing I can do. A noise, half-scream, half-groan, comes out of someone's mouth. Someone else yells, "Deirdre!"

My whole body buzzes and throbs. The metallic smell of blood and gunpowder is everywhere. "Shit," I hiss, as bullets fly into the room and puncture the walls. Tears are blurring my vision.

"Cease fire! Cease fire!" shouts Helicon into his megaphone. "This doesn't have to go this way!"

"You cease fire," yells Augur. "There are women and children in here!"

But no one ceases. The shooting continues from both sides. I hear another shout from outside, and then the front door flies open, and Augur and Uncle Hiram stumble back inside, bullets flying past them. Somebody kicks the door closed again.

I haven't eaten. I haven't had any water. It's been at least four hours now since the shooting started. I don't think I've taken a breath since.

Uncle Holden's body is lying on the porch; Aunt Deirdre's is here inside, a coagulating pool of blood around her head. As far as I know, they're the only ones we've lost, but I haven't left this room, so it's possible there are others. I don't know where Sami is—a thought that makes me sick. But I haven't heard about any children being lost yet. There are whispers we've killed a few of them, too, which, despite knowing what they've come here for, makes me feel guilty.

I can still taste the tang of my morning breath, and my nightgown is damp with sweat and there's a spatter of Aunt Deirdre's blood on one sleeve. I'm lying on my stomach on the floor, clutching my rifle like it's a branch that's keeping me from being swept down a raging river. Allison lies next to me. She keeps asking me if this is really happening, saying, "I just want this to be over."

Helicon makes another announcement, pleading with us for all the children to be released, promising that they won't be hurt.

My eyes dart to Aunt Deirdre's body in the corner. *Too late for her,* I think.

Augur disappeared upstairs hours ago, which felt a bit like abandonment, but when he comes back down, I'm so happy to see someone in authority that I don't even care. He's carrying a wireless microphone and portable speaker.

Through the closed door, he announces that he's coming out again and that he's unarmed. He waits until the shooting stops. It's followed by an eerie silence. I soak it up in case it never comes back. Augur opens the door.

What follows is a long back-and-forth negotiation on the number of children he'll release. It's excruciating to listen to: it's our lives that they're bargaining over like this is all a big game. In the end, Augur settles on releasing seven of us, "but only if the shooting stops now and forever."

Seven? Only seven? We've got at least twenty in that basement. There's got to be at least forty of us in total.

Helicon pleads with him to release more, but Augur has drawn the line. "Seven children at noon. That's my final offer."

Please. Take it. Some of them must get out of here.

There's a deafening silence from outside.

"All right. We'll have everything ready for them in twenty minutes."

Augur steps back inside and closes the door. He walks over to the basement door and looks down the stairs. "Jenifer, Thomas, and Edward." He turns to examine the room. "Eve, Michel, Yotam, and Kelly."

He could send us all out. He could. There are so many little kids in that basement. He could send all of them out if he wanted. But he won't. Why? Eve is crying and clinging to Dawn. Is he really going to separate twins? It's sadistic.

Someone say something! Please!

But no one has the courage. Aunt Haley, Fawn, and I help the little ones get into fresh clothes. All three have wet themselves. I hug Jenifer tightly. Summer is nowhere to be seen. Augur, after picking the seven children, has gone back upstairs. I know Sami is alive somewhere, but I haven't seen her.

When I leave the kids' room, Allison hands me a note, frantically whispering, "Tell Yotam to give it to Helicon."

I unfold it and quickly read it.

FBI, ATF, whoever you are. Help us get out - Allison, Kyle, and Juniper Green.

I give Yotam a hug right before I lead him over to the six other children and whisper in his ear, "Yotam, I need you to do something really important for me, okay?" He nods his curly head, and I show him the folded note, then slip it in the pocket of his jeans. "When you go outside, there's going to be someone in black clothes waiting for you. Once you start walking with him, I want you to count to ten, and when you get to ten, hand him this. Okay?" He nods yes, but when he looks at me I can see the fear in his eyes. I try not to show my own. It isn't easy. "Can you do that for me, Yotam?"

He nods. I squeeze him harder, and release him to Aunt Haley, who smiles over at me, as if she knows what I'm up to.

The shooting has stopped, and we're finally able to do things like go to the bathroom and eat. Like always, there's hardly anything in the cupboard—just crackers and rice cakes—but we're so hungry it doesn't matter. Everyone is afraid to make any noise. We talk a little, quietly, no one saying anything much of consequence. Sami and I exchange an empty look as we pass in the hall.

I still haven't seen Summer.

Aunt Jane tells me to get some rest. I would love to, or even just get changed. I'm rung out, exhausted beyond belief, but I can't imagine falling asleep. My nightgown has a sharp, nearly animal smell, but I hardly notice it, because everything and everyone in here smells like that.

Sami and I haven't exchanged a single word since this started. I wish I'd put my name with Allison's, Kyle's and Juniper's. I just want out of here. Now.

The bathroom is my only refuge. I shut myself in and sit on the closed toilet lid, just so I can have a few seconds to breathe.

Is this what the end of the world feels like?

Does it feel like someone squeezing your lungs, head and heart? Augur said it wouldn't be easy, but he never told us it would be like this. I imagined us all going to heaven in one explosive moment, but here we are, stuck in this nerve-fraying slow-motion war zone, this purgatory. I can't think of anything worse than this.

There's a knock on the bathroom door.

"Occupied," I say.

The lockless door swings open.

"Hey, are you deaf? There's someone in here—"

It's Fawn. She closes the door behind her, then slides down the wall next to me, putting her head on her knees, crying softly.

I search for something comforting to say but can't think of anything. *At least it'll be over soon? We'll be rewarded in heaven?*

Would hearing that be comforting in the slightest?

I opt for putting my hand on Fawn's shoulder.

"I'm so scared, Gracie," she says. "I don't want to die."

I wish I had something wise to say to her, but I don't.

All I can do is hold her hand and pray that neither of us is going to die tonight.

Now

I'm not sure what I expected would happen.

I don't know if I thought Sami would slap me, kiss me, or just turn around and leave. But for her to look calmly at me and say, "Hi," was kind of the last thing I envisioned.

"Hi," I say back, voice shaking slightly.

She shifts in the doorway, folding her arms across her chest.

Her short hair is in a ponytail, and a scar stretches from her eyebrow to her hairline. How she got that, I don't even want to know. Some of the kids do have violent streaks. But then again, so does Sami. Her hands must have gotten burned; the skin is pink like a baby's. Like Fawn despite the scars, she looks healthy, happy even. And she's still Sami.

"Um, can we like, talk—" She tilts her head in the direction of the hall.

"Sure," I say, trying to pretend that my heart isn't beating fifty times a second. I stand up and walk out the door with her. We walk a few steps in silence, then she stops abruptly. Behind her, the walls are painted a blinding shade of white.

"So. You came," Sami says, not making eye contact.

"I came."

She bites her lip, trying to find the right words. "I'm sorry about Summer."

"I'm sorry about your parents."

"They got what they wanted. Hopefully, they're in heaven," she says.

There are a million stupid things I want to tell her. I want to tell her I bought a book I thought she would like at a gas station convenience store; and that her hair looks pretty this way; and that I miss her; that when I'm awake in the dead of night, she's all I can think about; that when I fall asleep, she's there too; that I wish things were different; that I'm so sorry for everything I did.

But I came here for a reason. To answer a question.

"I came... I came to ask you about this—I mean, that's not the only reason I came, but I wanted to ask..." I pull the printed picture from my pocket and hand it to her.

I watch as she unfolds the paper and can't help noticing how pink her fingertips are. She lets out a strangled gasp. "What is this? Where did you find this?" she asks.

"The internet," I say. "And I just... I needed to know why."

"Why what?" She doesn't lift her eyes from the paper.

"Well, I mean, it's a lot of different stuff—I remember so little from that day, anyway. But mostly, why are you smiling? In the picture, I mean."

She looks up at me, anger in her eyes. "Why do you think?"

"I—"

"I can't believe I thought you came back because you cared about me."

"Sami, I do care." My voice cracks.

"Then act like it. Don't ask stupid fucking questions." She throws the picture to the ground and stomps off.

I stand there, mouth agape, eyes burning with tears.

Nice going. What did you really think was going to happen? That she'd just tell you everything on the spot? That she wouldn't freak out? You really are stupid.

"So, so stupid," I whisper to myself.

Nathan and Lauren went for a drive, so I have to wait in the lobby sitting area for them to come back.

Five minutes pass.

Sami never came back to see me again, and when I ask for her room number, they won't give it to me. I try not to show how desperate I am.

Ten minutes.

I am, though.

Fifteen minutes.

"Gracelyn?" The receptionist stands in front of me, smiling. "I have something for you."

I raise an eyebrow. She has her hands behind her back.

"It's a little present from Sami." She winks at me as if to convey a joke. Then she holds out a paper bag. "Happy reading." Then she walks back to her desk, watching me out of the corner of her eye.

I open the bag and remove a note from inside.

Here's why, genius.

The other thing in the bag is a thick letter, almost bursting out of the envelope.

"Hey, sorry we're late. Ready to go?" Lauren's standing over me. "Dad's waiting in the car."

I shove everything back into the crinkled bag and look up at her.

"You okay?" she asks.

"Yeah, yeah."

All you ever do is lie to this girl.

I stand up and give her a forced smile. She smiles back and we walk out to the car.

Back at the hotel, lying on my half of the bed that I'm sharing with Lauren, I open Sami's letter.

Dear Gracelyn,

I'm really mad at you right now. You know that, but I'm going to spell it out so you stop feeling sorry for yourself. And I know you just want answers, but that makes me angry too. You've always been so much luckier than me. You don't see it this way, but you're lucky you can't remember. Remembering hurts more. So I'm going to tell you what happened. Because I don't want to be mad at you forever, and I don't think we can get along anymore if you don't know what I know. And because I am still mad, maybe I want to hurt you with what happened. I don't know.

There was a fire. There was you. I'm sorry for cutting off your hair, by the way. I figured it wouldn't set on fire if it was shorter, which is stupid in hindsight. I didn't set the fire, but I knew about it a little bit beforehand. It was probably Augur, but I can't prove that. I overheard people talking about the fire, and I just knew I had to help you, stop him, save myself. I couldn't get you out of there with me, you would have wanted to go back for Summer. And I knew she probably wasn't going to want to go...

Sixteen Years Before

T anya stepped out of the car and stretched. Her husband reached into the backseat and helped their daughter out of the car. "Some drive, huh Summa-lum?"

While Doug unloaded their bags and Summer ran circles around the green pickup truck, Tanya walked away from the fence they had parked next to and toward the towering chapel.

She noticed a garden full of fresh vegetables. At home, the vegetables they bought from the produce section at the A&P were tasteless. Potatoes that looked like chalk inside and mushy, flavorless tomatoes. But just to look at them, she knew the vegetables in this garden tasted perfect. Tanya would have to bring Nathan out here someday soon. He'd really love it here.

For a group that the evangelist made seem so large, there was almost no one outside, and there was just one big residential building. *Things must be cozy in there*, she thought, turning her attention back to the chapel. Just as she reached the front steps, she heard someone shouting behind her.

"Hey there, Miss, you lookin' for Randolph?" A man with salt-and-pepper hair wearing a tight white t-shirt was jogging toward Tanya, sweating profusely. "He said some folks were headed here, but he didn't mention they'd be this pretty."

Tanya blushed, flattered. "I'm Tanya. Nice to meet you."

"Hiram. Do you need help with your bags?"

"My husband can handle it, I think."

"Where are you guys from? Was it much of a drive?"

Tanya walked down the steps to shake the hand Hiram held out to her. "Well, originally I'm from New Jersey, but me and Doug moved out west when our daughter was born."

"Hey babe, who's this?" Doug was walking toward them with their bags in one arm and Summer in the other. When he held their daughter like that, Tanya felt a beautiful ache in her chest. She had married such a good man.

"This is Hiram. He's going to show us around."

"Nice to meet you, Doug."

The four of them walked away from the chapel and toward the building Tanya assumed they would be moving into. "You caught us right in the middle of lunch or else this place would be bustling, let me tell you," Hiram said, motioning around the big empty yard. "We've got almost a hundred members now. Randolph really speaks to people—you'll see."

"I hope so," Doug said, chuckling. "Or else we just drove four hours out here for nothing." Tanya and Hiram laughed, and Summer laughed too, which made the adults laugh even harder. The door swung open, and Tanya almost gasped.

There were, as Hiram said, almost a hundred people sitting at four long tables. They were all chatting, laughing, and eating brown rice. Tanya hated brown rice, but that was beside the point. She noticed a toddler who looked similar in age to Summer, with food all over his face.

Doug whistled. "You weren't kidding, Hiram, this is a lot of people."

"Oh yeah, well, I wouldn't worry about space. It's a squeeze, but we manage." Hiram took a few steps into the dining room. "Has anyone seen Augur?" he shouted out to the crowds.

"Augur?" Doug mouthed to Tanya, smiling. She shrugged.

Suddenly, a man not much younger than her little brother appeared at the foot of the long staircase. "Hey there! You must be Tanya and Doug. So nice to meet you both. I'm Randolph."

After unpacking their bags and talking to more friendly souls than they could count (or remember) and introducing Summer to Elizabeth and some of the other toddlers, Tanya and Doug finally had a moment to themselves.

"Babe?" Doug asked as they made their new bed.

"Yeah?"

"Are we sure about this? Is this the greatest idea? I know this guy's message really speaks to you. It speaks to me, too. But we uprooted our whole lives to come here. I don't know if this is really what we've been missing. Up until recently, I feel like you weren't even that religious—"

Tanya walked to the other side of the bed and took hold of his hands. "Hey, hey, relax. I think this is perfect. Summer will have all these new friends. Randolph seems nice. It might take some getting used to, but I think this will be good for us. I want to get closer to God. And anyway, we can always leave. We're not trapped here."

Doug sighed. "Yeah, I know. You're right."

Tanya kissed her husband's hands. "Well, of course. I'm always right."

January Fifteenth

I wake up from a restless sleep, coughing.

I can't see a thing at first.

Dark smoke billows underneath and around the door, and I keep coughing, waving my arms around, trying to chase away the darkness. Eyes stinging, half-blind, I feel something strange and, squinting, I see that the braids that were once attached to my head now lie at the foot of my bed, like some sort of twisted peace offering. Who did that to me? Women aren't allowed to get haircuts. Everyone knows that. I'm coughing so hard now it hurts.

Panic sets in.

I roll out of bed, onto the floor, some instinct telling me to stay low. Covering my mouth and nose with a hand to block out the smoke, I peer around the room, trying to see if there's anyone else still in here.

Juniper and Kyle are pushing aside furniture, trying to get to our windows. Kyle has thrown Allison over his shoulder, but she isn't moving. *Oh, God.*

The younger kids are under the beds, coughing and pulling their shirts over their noses. Some of them are completely still. Scarily still. I don't see Sami anywhere.

The fire must be out there in the main room.

Kyle has reached the window, and he starts punching it, he knows that it doesn't open on its own. His knuckles weep with blood, but he's able to shatter the glass and climbs through. Allison's head hits the window frame as he pulls her body through. A few of the more alert kids run after him, and Juniper helps them through. She tries shouting at the rest of them, but either they can't hear her or they're already dead. The realization makes me shiver. They're all so young. Too young to die. Too young...

Come on, idiot, move! Do you *want to die?*

I try to make my way to the window, but my feet won't let me. I don't see Sami here. I need to find her. We've said a lot of stupid things, but I'm not leaving without her.

Out the door I go, plunging into the thick cloud of smoke that lies beyond, holding the collar of my nightgown over my nose but coughing uncontrollably, anyway. Shouting vainly for Sami and summer in between coughs.

I haven't seen any actual fire yet, but when I reach the main room, I can see flames darting from under the door of the men's quarters. Screaming. Loud and guttural, more animal than human. People running around, scratching the walls for an escape. I hear gunshots, screams, thuds.

I step forward and my foot hits something soft. It's Aunt Jane on the ground, a hole in the side of her skull spilling blood, a gun grasped in her hand, mouth twisted into a weird, peaceful smile.

My stomach lurches. *This is sick. This is so bad.*

Then I see him. He's with Summer, emerging from the smoke like apparitions, hand in hand.

Augur says something to her, and she rushes through the crowd, toward me. More gunshots. More thuds.

Augur steps around bodies, digs into his pants pocket, pulling something from it, then slips out the back door. The back door that the government locked along with all the others. According to him. Does no one else see him?

I grab onto Summer's arm as she approaches. "Summer," I cough.

She shakes my hand off. "Stand still." She pulls her gun from its holster and presses it into the side of my head. "This is better."

The metal is cold and hard against my temple. For a second, the chill I feel from its touch is almost nice, the air is so suffocating and hot.

"Summer..." I say. There are five million things I want to say to her, but her name is the only thing I can get out.

"Grace, you and I, we're going to ascend together. We'll finally get our reward. We've been so good we deserve this."

"Summer, stop. I don't want to die. Please." I cough again, the smoke filling the room faster and faster by the second. Flames lick the walls.

"It's not a death," Summer says. Tears brim in her eyes, either from smoke or emotion, I can't tell. "It's Augur's plan is for us. That's all that's ever mattered."

Oh God, I'm actually going to die. My sister is going to kill me.
"It's going to be okay, Grace."
She cocks the gun.
Come on, idiot. You don't want to die this way.
Not before finding Sami.
I swing my arm around suddenly, hitting the gun as hard as I can. It flies out of her hand and slides across the floor, coming to rest against Uncle Wes's corpse. Before she can react, I dive for it, rolling over and grabbing it by the butt.
"Back up," I yell, pointing it at her.
She doesn't move.
"Back the fuck up, Summer."
She takes a step backward, coughing while she does.
"You can do it, Grace. I'm ready."
The look on her face makes me feel so empty. She wants to die. She *wants* to die. She wants me to do this.
"I'm not going to kill you, Summer. I can't do that."
I see a flicker of emotion in her eyes, and she reaches out. "Grace—"
Suddenly, the ceiling creaks and groans, crumbling near the door to the kids' quarters. I jump sideways as debris rains down. "We've got to get out of here."
Summer looks toward the windows behind me, coughing again, almost convulsively. She gasps, "The kids in the basement," taking another step toward me. "Grace, we have to help them."
I'm afraid to lower the gun, afraid of what she'll do if she gets her hands on it again. Keeping the barrel leveled at her, I step toward the door and try to open it. The handle won't turn. It's locked. I look back at Summer and shake my head. The smoke is still billowing into the room, thicker and darker than before.
"Okay. One of us has to go outside and find Augur. He must have the keys, right?" I glance at the back door. The door Augur used.
Summer seems too done in by the smoke to respond, and there's no more time to waste. I run past her, throwing the gun as hard as I can at one of the windows, which shatters, the gun landing outside somewhere, out of her reach.
Scrambling out the back door into daylight, I suck in fresh air. Miraculously, there's no one around, though I can hear the deafening chuff of helicopter

blades overhead. I take off on a dead run toward the chapel, the only place he could have gone—the only building not on fire.

I don't know much about what Augur keeps in the chapel, but I know there are a lot of guns in there.

Not that there's anyone left to use them.

When I reach the row of windows and the door at the back, I cup my hands to look inside.

Augur is in there, holding matches, with a can of gasoline sitting where the bible usually does. He's leaning against the lectern, almost casually.

Just as I'm about to open the back door, I hear the front door open and see Sami run in, breathing hard. I hear her strangled gasp when she sees Augur standing there. "You," she says, more angry than I've ever heard her. She's got a gun that she's pointing straight at Augur's chest.

My heart pumps a rush of blood that catches somewhere in my throat.

"Hello, Samira. Why don't you put the gun down?" I can't see Augur's face, but in his deliberate calmness, he actually sounds scared.

"No."

"Samira, you don't want to kill me." He steps forward, and she steps back. "Why would you do that to your family?"

"My family is dead. You killed them all."

"I did no such thing. If people have died, it's because they gave their lives over to God, as we all must."

"Bullshit. *Bullshit.* You made them think they had to do something like that."

He must notice that she's moving backward, so he takes a few more steps forward. She might have a gun, but he still has the power.

I don't know what to do. She needs my help. I know I have to help her. But I'm frozen.

"They believed in me, and now they'll be rewarded. How can you fault them for that? Are you that selfish?" He continues to move forward. She's practically pressed against the door. "Your mother would be disappointed in you, my dear. You used to be such a good girl, and now look at you. Pointing that gun at me."

I open the door a crack. It squeaks, but he doesn't even notice. I don't think Sami notices, either.

"Your mother believed in what was right. She died happy, and you, because you are an angry, sinful child, will die unhappy, angry, and alone—"

"Shut up!" Sami fires a shot over his head, which splinters the wooden ceiling.

Augur takes a step back.

"You don't know the first thing about me," Sami says. "I never, ever, for one second believed you and all your horseshit. I know what it's like to feel 'happy,' and you were wrong about it all. You really think you're a God, don't you? That's pathetic. You're just a man. A horrible, disgusting, evil man. And I am not going to listen to you for one more fucking second!"

I can't see what he's doing, even though I've stepped into the chapel proper. Sami is so focused on him, she hasn't even glanced my way.

I pick the gas can off the lectern.

I run forward with the can and smash it into the back of his head as hard as I can. For a split second, before he falls to the ground, I see the lit match in his hand and the keys on his belt. Then he crumples, and the flames ignite.

"Gracie?" Sami says, as the flames spread across the entire floor and all the pews. She stumbles backward, coughing from all the smoke.

I reach down and take off Augur's belt, yanking it out of the loops and clutching the keys in my gas soaked hand. He groans in protest. When I look back up, Sami is on her hands and knees.

The flames are climbing the walls. Dark smoke clouds every inch of my vision. I climb over Augur and grab Sami by the arm, dragging her toward the door. I turn the knob and kick the door open, inhaling every bit of the fresh air that I can.

I can't even tell if Sami's still breathing.

I drag her off the porch and away from the toxic air that's spilling out of every window. She's still got the gun clutched in her hand.

"Hands in the air! Right now!" Two black-clad ATF agents run toward us, assault weapons leveled, their voices loud and terrifying.

I ignore them, continuing to pull Sami away from the chapel.

"On the ground! Now!"

"The kids!" I stop and hold up the belt. "They're in the basement. The keys, I have the keys! Please!"

One of the agents swoops in and takes the belt out of my hand, then hustles away toward the main building. I can hear him yelling at the others, "The basement! The kids are in the basement!"

The other one just stands there, gun trained on me.

"She's hurt," I yell at him. "She needs help."

"Shut up," he says, without moving. Behind him, I can see the only home I've ever known, engulfed in flames.

The agent who took the keys emerges from the wall of smoke, looking somber and shell-shocked. There are no children with him. Not a single one.

Before I can even think about what that means, there's an explosion in the chapel. Fire tears through its roof and, as I watch, the wooden structure is completely engulfed in flames, the intensity of the heat so powerful that my cheeks burn.

Now

I finish reading Sami's letter, some of the ink smearing because my fingers are wet from wiping away tears.

Of course, she pointed that gun at him.

It would have been so satisfying to watch him, the person who ruined our lives before they even started, destroyed by something so small.

Of course, she's smiling in that picture.

She was free. We were free.

It's not just her words that are making my hands shake, but the memories going off like flashbulbs in my brain.

Blood on the ground, under my bare feet. Bodies holding other bodies. Little kids choking to death on smoke under beds where only make-believe monsters are supposed to lurk. Sami's eyes filled with fear. Augur's last words.

Summer's hand shaking—but not shaking nearly enough—as she pressed the gun against my temple. The sound of her final cough, which sounded like something was trying to escape her body.

I remember it all. How I couldn't see. How each breath stung. The relief and elation of getting out into the air. How Kyle's knuckles bled as he punched through a window to save the girl he loved. How badly my head hurt.

So many things going through my mind. How my first thought with the cold metal of a gun pressed to my skull was of Sami. How moments after watching her do the worst thing she ever did, I tried to save her. How she summed up our whole lives in a few choice words to the man who did his best to destroy us: "I know what it's like to feel happy, and you were wrong about it all. You really think you're a God, don't you? That's pathetic. You're just a man. An evil, disgusting little man."

I'm not sad anymore, but I can't stop crying. Mostly, I'm angry. Really, really angry.

I'm mad at Sami for not telling me the truth about how he treated her, for letting me think she was dead, for keeping secrets and not telling me how she felt. Didn't she know telling me would have made me feel less alone?

I'm angry with my parents for going to the compound in the first place.

I'm angry with Summer for hurting me at every turn. For choosing him over me. For lying to me. For being willing to kill me. And then for leaving me.

I'm angry at Augur. For creating a world where he was king and the rest of us suffered. For making me feel like I had to hide. I'm angry at him for everything he ever said. I only wish I had been able to see his face when that match hit the floor.

Above all, I'm angry with myself. For the way I've behaved. For being so easily influenced. For hurting people who have cared about me. For being cruel to Nathan and Dr. Yen, who just wanted to help me. For scaring Lauren. For forgetting and letting myself forget. For remembering.

Somehow, remembering feels a lot like a death.

Zombie-like, I make way into the hotel room bathroom and lock the door.

Nathan's cologne bottle is on the counter. A water glass sits on a tiny porcelain dish. I pick up the cologne and smash it on the tiled bathroom floor. It shatters into a million shards of sickly sweet-smelling glass. I do the same thing with the dish. Then the cup.

I sweep my arms across the counters and knock everything to the floor. I scream as if I'm being murdered. I don't care. I just don't care.

There's a frantic knocking on the door, worried voices.

"Gracelyn? Are you all right?"

Really? Isn't it clear I'm not all right? That no one is ever *all* right? That there's always something wrong?

Everyone's been telling me I'm getting better. But what does that even mean?

Did they expect me to just become a different person the moment I stepped off the compound? I'm the same person I always was.

My screams have turned into spasmodic jerking hiccups, and I can't seem to stop them. I slump down on the damp shower floor, put my head in my arms, and try to breathe.

The bathroom door opens.

A warm body slides in next to me. "How did you get in?"

"Hotel rooms use really basic locks in their bathrooms," Lauren says. "Just put some scissors in the keyhole and twist. Learned that at camp." She puts a hand on my shoulder. Then she wraps both arms around me. "I'm sorry."

"I know."

She pulls me closer, and I let her.

Someone else comes in the bathroom. "Dad, be careful, there's glass—"

"Ah!" Nathan says. I peek up from my arms and look at him. He's hopping around, holding his bloody foot. The cut isn't that deep, but it *looks* bad.

"Are you okay?" Lauren asks him.

"Well," I interject. "Obviously not."

We're all silent for a second, and then Lauren giggles. Then Nathan starts. Soon, we're all laughing, and Nathan even has to wipe away tears. He kneels down and puts his arms around us both, and I lean cautiously into him.

"I'm sorry about your cologne."

"It's okay. That stuff smells awful anyway."

Lauren giggles again. Then we all go quiet.

"I'm so fucking tired," I say.

"I know, kid, I know." Nathan holds us a little tighter and kisses the top of my head. "It's exhausting, isn't it? This business of being alive."

I smile into his arm. Lauren gets closer to me, and the three of us huddle together, taking comfort in each other's warmth.

Now

"Hello?" Sami's voice drifts through the phone.

"It's Gracelyn."

She says nothing.

I take a deep breath. "Randolph Milly was born on April second, nineteen eighty, in New Mexico. That makes him an Aries, apparently."

"A what?"

"His father was in jail most of his childhood, and his mother raised him alone. He claimed she beat him, but she hasn't publicly confirmed this. The two of them didn't go to church regularly, but he went with his devout grandmother, who said that for a child he was uncharacteristically interested in the scriptures. He read the Bible for fun and made up his own ideas about it from a young age."

"Gracelyn—"

"He was an average high school student," I continue. "He wasn't ever invested in academics but excelled in music class. Not because of raw talent, but because he was passionate about it. Teachers and his mother occasionally caught him doing drugs, and he had his driver's license suspended at nineteen for drunk driving and never got it back. There's no proof he ever went to college. At twenty, he married a woman named Vera Munch. The marriage certificate listed her age as eighteen, but in fact she was only sixteen.

"This was about that time he got involved with the Church of the Holy Saviors. After becoming the leader, he began openly sleeping with other women. Vera Munch left, and though she reportedly never had any children with him, one of the children living in the compound was named Vera, and Milly claimed her as his own. He quickly recovered from Vera's departure, taking Jane Morehouse as his second wife." I look up from the article I've been reading. "And I think you know how the rest of the story goes."

A pause. Then a loud sigh. "Why are you telling me this?"

"Because you were right. When you said that he was just a man. He was just a man who existed, who did a lot of horrible things. And we killed him."

Silence.

"We didn't mean to, but we did. We burned down the building he was in, and I'm not saying that to make you feel bad because I know you must already feel a little guilty, or a lot guilty. I just say it because I've been thinking about us. About how angry we both are. You were smiling in that picture because you were finally free of the things that made you angry. And I'm sorry for asking you about it. People asked me about that kind of thing, too, and it made me freak out, so I don't blame you."

Sami clears her throat and says, "So you read the letter?"

"Yes..."

"I'm glad."

Silence.

"The whole thing?"

"Yeah."

"It wasn't boring?"

"Are you kidding?"

We get quiet again. I'm imagining putting my hand on her shoulder.

"I—" Sami mumbles something.

"What?"

"I—I realize that twice you've told me you love me, and I didn't say it even once. So even though things have changed, and even if we aren't together forever or anything, I need to tell you I love you, too. A lot. And I'm sorry. For what I said—and what I didn't say." She pauses. "Also, that I cut your hair. It was weird logic."

Miracle of miracles, I manage to laugh. "It's okay, I like it." It takes everything in my power to keep myself from crying. "I'm sorry too."

"He didn't try to get out, you know."

I sniff back the tears. "What?"

"We never locked the door. He wasn't unconscious. I'm pretty sure he could have escaped the building if he'd really wanted to. Maybe he just... didn't."

"Maybe."

"I guess we'll never know."

"Sami," I say, feeling like this is as good a time as any to bring it up. "I want to invite you on a field trip. Nathan already asked the people at the ward about it."

"A field trip?" she asks. "Are we going to a field?"

"No, that was confusing for me, too."

"Are you *absolutely* sure this is a good idea?" This is the seventh time Lauren's asked during the car ride, and the fifteenth time since she learned about the idea. Sami and the nurses are in a big black car behind us.

"Yes, Lauren. This is a good idea."

"I wouldn't be so sure about that," says Nathan. His hands are gripping the wheel so tightly his knuckles have gone white.

"Can you two please calm down?" I say, staring out the window at the increasingly familiar road. "I don't know if it's a good idea or not, but believe me, you're not making it better by being so tense."

After a few minutes of driving, we're stopped by two black-clad men at a checkpoint, and in the distance, I can see the remains of what I once called my home.

Nathan gets out of the car and talks to them. They glance at me, and at the black car behind us, and then nod. Nathan looks back and waves us over.

We unfasten our seatbelts and go to join him. Lauren grabs my hand as we walk past the guards. Sami and her escorts follow us. Little dust clouds billow around our feet with each step.

At the gate, I look at Sami. She takes my other hand.

We all step through the gate together.

Now

*O*nce upon a time there was a little girl named Summer.

The chapel is completely destroyed, but the main building is still standing, and the front door is wide open. Yellow caution tape is wrapped around the charred shell. Nathan, Lauren, and the nurses hang back to let me and Sami go in on our own first. There are burn marks on the ground, piles of ash everywhere.

"Keep it together," Sami mumbles.

I nod, taking another deep breath.

When Summer was very young, her parents took her to live in the desert with a Magician. A bit later, her mother went away to have another baby. Her new sister came home but her mother didn't.

The inside of the building is like charcoal. There's rubble everywhere. I feel my chest tighten, and I squeeze Sami's hand tighter. She squeezes back.

Everyone told her that she should take care of her little sister now, that it was her job. No one else was going to help her when her father suddenly left. The Magician told her it was because her father didn't love her anymore, and Summer believed him.

I look at the basement door and my stomach turns. From Sami's face, I can see she feels the same way. Almost by habit, I head toward the kids' quarters. When we step inside, tears spring to my eyes again. Sami's sniffling, too.

As she got older, Summer took care of her sister as best as she could, and tried to live a good, holy life. The Magician kept telling her that she had grown to be quite beautiful. She didn't particularly like that, but all the other women told her she should be happy with the attention. She began to tell herself that she was.

I'd almost forgotten what this room looked like. I turn, taking in every burnt inch of the walls. It all rushes back. *God.* The way the sheets smelled. The pink curtains on the girl's side, the blue curtains on the boy's side. The laughter that echoed in the halls, less and less of it as I got older. The sunlight reflecting on the mirror, where I watched my body get thin, weak, and bruised as the years went on. The grimy way my hair felt within hours of washing it. The way my skin peeled away from my nose, and the permanent red color of my cheeks. Sami lying next to me, curled against my back while I shook in the middle of the night. Tracing the mark Summer's hand left on my face, and thinking, *this is the first time she's touched me in years.*

The bed frames are charred. I suppose the fire was out before they could burn completely. Nathan prepared me for all the mattresses to be gone. Apparently, they needed DNA from them to identify bodies. But seeing the empty bed frames hits me hard. It's like we were never here.

When she was fifteen, Summer woke up bleeding. The bed was soaked with her blood, and she started to scream. All the women told her it was the best thing ever to happen to her. After a while, she started to believe them. And they told the Magician, who gave her a speech about her duty as a woman, a scary smile on his face the whole time.

I look at my bed, at the bottom bunk of my bed, which Jenifer had just started sleeping in a week or two before the raid. Sami stands in the middle of the room, not touching anything, not saying anything. She tugs anxiously on her ponytail. I notice that if it were down, her hair would be uneven on both sides. Maybe I can get Lauren to fix it one day.

A few days after she woke up bleeding, the magician asked her to marry him. She was happy, or so she told herself. She was worried about her sister, but the magician reminded her that the only thing that mattered now was him and the children they would have together. Summer thought that she was too young to have children, but she was married now, and she had to do whatever he told her to do.

"Can you believe we spent our whole lives in here? I can't really remember what it looked like before," Sami says. "I don't remember a lot of things."

"I remember," I say. I stare at my empty bed. I remember falling asleep to the sound of Allison and Juniper gossiping. I remember helping Fawn tuck in the younger kids. I remember being tucked in by Aunt Elizabeth and Summer.

I remember going to Summer's bed during storms, and how, after she moved upstairs, I just had to try and sleep but never could. Sami grabs my arm and turns me around. She holds my head in her hands and shakes me a bit. I only realize I'm crying when I see her wet fingers.

"Gracie, stay with me, okay?"

When he finally did give her a baby, Summer was happy. When she gave birth to her daughter, it was the most painful, horrible thing she had ever experienced. She thought that her sister cared more than that, but the Magician told her she hadn't even bothered to show up. She thought she remembered her sister being there at some point, but she had to believe the Magician. He and her daughter were all that mattered now. Not Grace.

"It's over," Sami assures me.

I stare into her eyes. They're beautiful, dark and deep, somewhere between copper and amber. It's been so hard not being able to look into her eyes. I pull her in for a hug, my tears darkening the shoulder of her shirt.

As the years went on, Summer was more and more drawn into what the Magician told her, until she believed that he was the only thing in the world that mattered. She did anything he told her. If he said it, it was true, and it was indisputable.

I almost think Sami is going to pull away, because it's pretty much the most inappropriate place for us to hug, but she doesn't. I realize that we're desperate for something to hold on to. We always have been.

"I don't want to be back here," I whisper to her.

"You don't have to," she replies.

We're broken, we're breaking, but we're together.

Maybe that's enough.

One night, the Magician told her she had to do something she didn't want to do. He handed her the knife but said it was up to her in the end. She loved him. She would do anything for him. So, she put on dark clothes and piled into the car with three others he trusted, and they sped away into the night.

Someone clears their throat; Sami and I break apart with a jump.

"Sorry to interrupt," Lauren says, standing in the doorway. She backs away slowly, the floorboards creaking under her feet. When she catches my eye, she waggles her eyebrows suggestively.

"We should see the rest of the building," I say quickly. Sami nods. We follow Lauren, hand in hand.

When Summer and the others arrived at their destination, she could hardly believe it. It was a house, not ten minutes away from their own, so obvious against the dusty night she was shocked they'd never seen it before. Hiram knocked on the door, and someone she didn't know answered. A man in his pajamas. Hiram nodded at her, and she pressed her knife to the man's throat.

"Say nothing."

The stairs are falling apart, and we climb them cautiously. One of the accompanying nurses gasps when Sami's foot goes through a step, but I manage to pull her out and we continue up to where the women's quarters and Augur's bedroom used to be. Names are sloppily painted on doors. Deirdre and Haley, Reina and Joy. Summer and Bridget.

I push open Summer's door and step inside. Sami and Lauren hang back, maybe understanding that I need to see this alone. Sami might want to see her mother's room too, as I hear their footsteps moving in that direction.

Summer held the man near the door while the others searched the house for Oliver and Gina. The Magician had told them the couple was dangerous, they had to be removed. Dan found Gina first. He roughly pulled her down the stairs by her hair and threw her to the floor.

Some of Gina's blonde hair was trapped in the flower clip that Dan ripped from her head.

I look around the room. It's small, like a tiny version of the kids' rooms downstairs. There are bunk beds in here, too. Summer's was the bottom one. I've never been in here before, but she was always scared of the top bunk. She must have been in the bottom one.

When we were little, she pulled up the floorboard under our bed and hid her possessions under it. She never let me see what they were, but maybe she did the same here. She's not around to stop me.

They brought Oliver down next and threw him to the floor near his "wife."

"Please," he begged. "Don't."

Dan didn't even hesitate. He brought the knife down on Oliver, and Gina let out a blood-curdling scream. So did the man in Summer's arms. He squirmed, but she pushed the blade even closer to the flesh of his neck.

Hiram leaned down and lifted Gina's head by her ear.

"Who do you work for?"

Most of the floorboards are loose and charred. I find the loosest one and try to pry it up, digging my bitten nails into the wood. When it suddenly gives way, I grunt and fall backward, clutching the board in my arms.

I crawl back toward the dark narrow cavity in the floor.

I'm prepared for anything but also not sure what I can handle seeing.

Gina's face gave away nothing. Though tears ran down her cheeks, she didn't shake or show any fear. She spat in Hiram's face. "I don't work for anyone."

"You lying bitch," he said, throwing her back to the ground. He wiped the spit off his face. "I've already killed your husband; you have nothing left to lose. But you seem to need some more incentive." He looked over at Summer. "Do it."

In the space under the floor, I find a photograph of Summer, Augur and Jenifer; a bracelet she made when we were younger; and a spool of thread. That's all.

Summer had a moment of panic. She couldn't kill this man. She didn't know him. He might be a disbeliever. But she didn't know for sure. All she knew was that he was a person, just like her. How could she kill him?

"Do it now!" Hiram screamed. "Do you want Augur to be angry with you?"

That was the only thing in the world that sounded worse than being a killer.

I don't know what I expected.

Maybe I expected a note, an explanation for why she hurt me, why she held a gun to my head, why she never loved me as much as I loved her, why she came home in the waking hours one morning covered in blood, and why she didn't fight for me.

I wanted to know that she cared. I wanted her to still be the sister I remembered. I wanted, I suppose, for her to be someone she wasn't anymore, and maybe never had been.

So she closed her eyes and slit open the throat of this man she'd never met. In front of a woman she'd once considered a friend.

Blood soaked her hands, her clothes. She dropped the limp body to the ground. Her hands shook. This was insane. This was wrong. But it was what the Magician wanted, so she tried not to breathe in the metallic smell of her crimes as she watched Gina bravely try to hold back her tears.

I rip the picture in half. Augur's head is split down the middle. Then I start to rip it until it's just shredded paper in my hands. Then I unravel the spool of thread. I continue to destroy the things my sister once held dear.

"Now, once again. Who do you work for?"

Gina stared back defiantly. "ATF." She looked around the room dramatically, then back at Hiram. "We already know about the illegal guns. And the statutory rape. But murdering two unarmed government agents? You're gonna fry for this, Hiram."

Hiram flushed red. He lifted his handgun. "You think that scares me? You think that's gonna help you get out of this house alive?"

When I'm finished unspooling the thread, I put the bracelet on my wrist.

Even after all of it, everything that happened, she was my sister. And no matter how hard I try, I can't change that. There will always be a piece of her in me. As much as I might wish that wasn't true.

Before I go, I put the cigarette the woman outside the supermarket gave me into the empty space the board had covered. I don't know why—maybe it feels like Summer could use a smoke. I stand up and walk out the door without looking back.

I think I'm done looking back.

They drove home in silence.

Summer was covered in blood, but not one thought passed through her head. She couldn't even force herself to think about what she'd just done. She could barely see.

Eight days later, she was dead.

It was almost felt like a relief.

Sami and Lauren are waiting in the hallway.

"I want to go home," I say. "Can we go home now?"

Eleven Months After

S ami says she's never liked anything more than she likes snow.

The two of are sitting on the steps of the U.S Capitol. It's been three hours since her parents' funeral, since Summer's funeral.

Sometimes when she comes to visit me in New Jersey, we sit on Nathan's porch, watching the snow. We bundle up in jackets and a blanket and sit on the porch swing for hours, just talking.

It's Christmas eve, and even though Nathan and Dr. Yen have put a ban on me getting within a hundred feet of a religious establishment, Lauren convinced them to let me see the parts of Christmas I had never seen before. She introduced me to some Dean Martin Christmas songs and made me hot chocolate and, of course, told me about snow. I had never seen it before I came to New Jersey. I had barely seen rain, for that matter. And now, snow is one of the many reasons I love waking up on the east coast every day.

Sami lives in Florida with her grandmother, where there also isn't any snow, but they came up to D.C for the funerals, and they're coming back to New Jersey with us for the holidays. Lauren and Sami are friends now, which is strange. It's like watching two people who don't have a common language but who somehow connect, anyway.

"What are you thinking about?" Sami asks, lifting her head from my shoulder.

"You."

"Hm. So the usual, then?"

"Pretty much."

She laughs. "I like that I'm still in your head."

"You're never leaving."

"Well, same here." Sami puts her head back on my shoulder. "What can I say? We're just very interesting."

I'd laugh under normal circumstances, but I guess I'm not in the mood.

The funeral was hard. There were no bodies to put in the ground. We didn't even pray. They just handed us little memorial plaques, so we could hang them in our living rooms or something. And yet I cried pretty much the whole time. Afterward, we all went out and got ice cream at Sami's grandmother's insistence. She's a super nice lady, though she doesn't really understand.

I look at Sami now. Her hair is short, face a little rounder, a little healthier. She still glows. She's still Sami.

We can see the Washington monument, slightly shrouded in winter fog and snow, towering over the reflection pool. "Do you remember how Aug—" I clear my throat. "—how Randolph used to say that was the tower of Babylon?"

"He also said it was a rocket filled with bombs, and one day it would launch and wipe out all the good Christians," Sami adds.

"Good times."

We still don't laugh. I look at her some more, so that I don't have to think about my sister's empty coffin being lowered into the frozen ground.

"Stop staring at me. You're making me self-conscious."

"Why? I'm staring at you because you're beautiful."

"Haha."

"I'm serious. I want to look at you all the time. Don't go home. Stay with me, so I can keep soaking up all that beauty."

"Gracie." Sami looks at me with an expression that makes me think she's scared for me. Or of me. "Just... let's be quiet."

"Okay." I take her hand.

We sit. Silence settles around us like the snow.

Soon, Nathan will bring the car around, and we'll go home and open presents and forget for too short a time everything that's happened. For now, though, we sit here together, quietly grieving and trying to make sense of the fact that we're still alive.

Sami squeezes my hand. I squeeze back.

I mean, here we are, covered in scars, head to toe. Some are visible. A lot are under the skin and still raw. Who knows if we'll ever heal completely?

After all that's happened, the biggest miracle of all is that we still have each other.

And I think we're going to be okay.

Acknowledgements

I have been writing and editing this book for almost three years. Along the way, I've had incalculable amounts of help.

Foremost, I want to thank my family. I could not have done this without my publisher/editor/father extraordinaire. Sorry for how testy I get with you, Dad. Without your help, I don't know if I'd have been able to turn what was sometimes a confusing mess into a book. So thank you! [*Editor's note: As much as I'd like to take credit, I must disagree.*]

I also want to thank my first and most important reader, my mom. Mom, you walked into my bedroom crying over the ending of this book, and that was the first time I knew it was good. Your advice is invaluable to me, and I love you.

And of course, thank you to my second test reader, my grandmother. You always have the best advice, Tata. Even when I don't listen to you, I always know that I probably should.

Thanks also to my friends (you know who you are). I'm sure almost all of you can see yourself in the character of Lauren, which I'm hoping you'll take as a compliment. Like Lauren, you've all taught me a lot about the world. I wouldn't be able to go on my weird journeys or adventures without you. This acknowledgment is mostly because I love you but also partly a bid to make sure that when you guys do read this you don't make fun of me too much.

And last, but not least, thank you to the wondrous Rachel Ake for the beautiful cover she designed. It looks amazing.

Author's Note

This is a true story. Or rather, it's the amalgamation of several true stories.

In 2020, I was looking for something to watch while riding out my last year of middle school online, and I came across a six-part YouTube series about the Manson Family. I watched the whole thing, and then I watched a documentary about the Branch Davidians, and then one about Jim Jones and Heaven's Gate. I couldn't get enough. Soon, I was tearing through novels about imaginary cults, watching hours-long documentaries with real footage of the Mount Carmel Compound burning down, reading *Helter Skelter*, and beginning to write this novel.

Gracelyn was a character who had knocked around in my head for a few years, and when I imagined her life, I began to wonder about what growing up in an environment like Mount Carmel might be like for a young girl my age.

The very particular world that Gracelyn grows up in borrows mostly from the true story of the Branch Davidians, a doomsday cult led by David Koresh in the 1980s and 1990s. But it also borrows elements from other American cults, like Jim Jones' People's Temple. One element I felt was important to retain from the People's Temple was their way of dealing with predatory and dangerous behavior within the temple—insular communities like these often try to deal with their bad apples from the inside, an approach that rarely works.

The part of my story that sticks closest to the historical accounts of the Branch Davidians is the end of the novel, namely the controversial events of

April 19th, 1993, when a fire broke out on the Davidians' compound after a 51-day standoff with the ATF. More than anything, I was trying to imagine and dramatize what that might have been like.

If you're interested in looking further into the true stories of these cults, I'd recommend *Helter Skelter* by Vincent Bugliosi and Curt Gentry; *Seductive Poison* by Deborah Layton; and *Armageddon: Critical Perspectives on the Branch Davidian Conflict*. I also recommend Stephanie Harlow's YouTube series.

Finally, I want to thank you for reading my book. I truly hope Gracelyn's story has meant as much to you as the telling of it has meant to me.

About the Author

Eden Alson is about to enter her senior year of high school in New York City. This is her second published novel. She was born in Brooklyn and now lives with her parents in Greenwich Village.